"I want you to think about exactly what you're facing.

"You already want to do something extraordinary, something very few skaters ever have the chance to do—to compete against the very best skaters in the country, maybe even the world."

Winnie quivered inside. Didn't he think she was good enough? He had said so, but now he was trying to discourage her.

"Think about it. None of the competitions you've ever been in, except nationals last year, can compare. It's hard. Not everyone can take the pressure."

Winnie sat back against her chair. "I did okay last year."

"That's another thing. You think you're good. You have the potential to be good, maybe even great. But you have no idea what I'm going to put you through these next six months. You may decide you hate me before we're done." He allowed himself to smile. "I won't be your friend. I can't even afford to like you. I have to teach you. I won't be Louise's brother. I'll be the former national champion who knows what it takes."

Winnie wanted him to be her coach and nothing more. Didn't she? Why was she hesitating?

Books by Darlene Franklin

Love Inspired Heartsong Presents

Hidden Dreams
Golden Dreams

DARLENE FRANKLIN

Award-winning author and speaker Darlene Franklin
lives in Oklahoma near her son's family.

Darlene loves music, needlework, reading and reality
TV. She has over twenty books published, including
three previous titles about Maple Notch, Vermont.
She's a member of both American Christian Fiction
Writers and Oklahoma City Christian Fiction Writers.

You can find Darlene online at
darlenefranklinwrites.blogspot.com
and www.facebook.com/darlene.franklin.3. You may
also be interested in her Facebook page, Darlene's
5 Questions a Day, where she will answer the first five
questions related to the writing life posed on any given
day. Group members are also welcome to contribute.

DARLENE FRANKLIN

Golden Dreams

HEARTSONG
PRESENTS

Recycling programs for this product may not exist in your area.

™ LOVE INSPIRED BOOKS

ISBN-13: 978-0-373-48672-4

GOLDEN DREAMS

www.LoveInspiredBooks.com

Printed in U.S.A.

For whatsoever is born of God overcometh the world: and this is the victory that overcometh the world, even our faith.
—*1 John* 5:4

Grandma took care of me while my mother worked to support us. At the age of seventy, she was baptized in the cold waters of Lake Maranacook in Winthrop, Maine, at the same time I was. She forced her fingers to learn piano as my nimble fingers danced their way through John Thompson's *Teaching Little Fingers to Play*.
I dedicate *Golden Dreams* and its heroine, Winnie Tuttle, to you, Grandma, aka Winifred Bremner.

Chapter 1

Saturday, July 4, 1931
Maple Notch, Vermont

Frank Sawtelle was home at last.

The people of Maple Notch, Vermont—Winnie Tuttle among them—had waited five years to give their hero a homecoming worthy of his accomplishments. Perhaps she'd anticipated his return even more than most. She leaned past Louise, seeking a glimpse of her friend's brother.

A matched pair of geldings as white as the stars on the United States flag pranced in front of a wagon decorated to resemble Fort Ticonderoga. A monument in the town square celebrated the American victory early in the Revolutionary War, when Maple Notch men fought alongside Ethan Allen and the Green Mountain Boys. When the horses swung their heads, golden plumes waved in the wind, suggesting the magic that Frank brought to the ice.

His skating had both mesmerized and charmed Winnie as an impressionable child.

Clean red-and-blue rugs were spread across the horses' backs, completing the patriotic theme. A man dressed like a Dickensian cabby, complete with top hat and scarf, held the long reins, driving the wagon fit for a king.

In spite of speculation that Frank would hide from public display, the man in the wagon stood at attention, saluting the cheering townsfolk. He wore the skating costume he'd worn five years ago, when he won the United States Figure Skating Championships: a copy of Ethan Allen's green uniform coat, faced with red, over buckskin breeches. Winnie recognized it because she had helped Louise and Mrs. Sawtelle sew it all those years ago. His hairstyle had changed, though. It was shorter and slicked back, but she loved the way he still filled out every inch of the coat.

He didn't look the least bit ill at ease with the festivities, as Louise had suggested he would. Winnie hopped from one foot to the other, waving her flag and yelling like everyone around her. Louise's little white mutt, Toodles, danced at their feet, feeding on the crowd's frenzy.

Frank turned almost-green eyes on her, smiled and waved his hand. The music and noise around her faded into the background, and she felt as if she were watching a movie, where the hero comes home to the woman who has faithfully waited.

High-pitched barking interrupted Winnie's private reverie. Toodles dashed across the street into the path of the horses. One stopped and the other lifted his front legs in the air, seeking to avoid the tiny animal. The crowd went silent.

"Do something!" a white-faced Louise begged Winnie.

Toodles huddled under the bed of the cart, where the tall wooden wheels would crush her if the wagon moved.

The driver fought to keep the horses under control. Winnie inched forward, one eye on the horses and the other on Toodles, to make sure the dog didn't make a dash for freedom. As she neared the vehicle, she saw that Frank had jumped down on the other side.

Toodles looked from one familiar face to the other, then ran past both of them to Louise and hopped into her arms, yipping.

At the sound, the crowd released nervous laughter. Frank straightened his jacket, replaced the black tricorn on his head and bowed before climbing back onto the wagon. He winked at Winnie and signaled for the driver to move forward.

Winnie melted back into the crowd and followed the parade until it turned the corner onto Old Bridge Road. After that, she stood still as children jostled and pushed past her.

Louise walked slowly forward, one hand clutching the dog to her chest, the other leaning on her cane. "What were you thinking? You could have been hurt. Bad Toodles." With the gentle scolding, she set the dog on the ground and waited a moment to catch her breath. "We'd better get moving. I want to thank Frank properly, and you'll have a chance to speak to him, too."

Am I that transparent? Heat rose to the roots of Winnie's hair. "Oh, I don't know. Everybody will want to say hello. He won't care about a nobody like me." Though he may have forgotten her, she had not forgotten him. Frank's return meant more than she dared share with anyone else, even Louise.

"Of course he will. You're my best friend. Especially when he learns you made the shortcake for his favorite dessert."

Winnie giggled at the suggestion. "Lucky for him strawberries are in season."

"I think that's why he came during the summer." Louise smiled and continued her slow progress down the street.

Louise was joking, of course, but Winnie knew the truth. A more serious reason than Maple Notch's desire to celebrate their hero had called Frank Sawtelle home. She took another look at her friend's face, paled by a prolonged bout with bronchitis that never seemed to improve, and linked their arms together. "Come. Let's get moving before all the good seats are taken."

At last the parade ended. Frank knew it hadn't lasted more than ten blocks. Why, in New York, his home in recent years, that short a distance didn't count at all. But today that mile felt more like they had traveled around Manhattan from Battery Park to the Upper East Side and back again. Maybe Maple Notch's mayor, who enjoyed spectacles and speechifying, enjoyed it. Frank sure didn't.

The wagon arrived at the city park only seconds ahead of the crowd. Frank jumped down and ran into the pavilion before anyone could see him. He had to get out of his costume before he burned up. He was no Ethan Allen, no hero, no matter what these people thought.

Frank had no desire to greet the clamoring crowd, not even people from his hometown. Especially not them; they had believed in him, all those years ago, and he had failed them.

The fans' faces had melded together over the years—boys who wanted to show him how good they were, girls who vied for his attention because he had won a medal, older matrons who fawned over him as if they had no husbands at home. He was allowing these people their moment. He had promised Mom and Dad he would cooperate.

On the ice, he forgot about everything and everyone. But at the job—the job he'd lost when the Depression had tightened its grip and the company shut its doors—he had been the token star, the man expected to entertain guests and bring in business.

Today, he had followed Dad's advice. Focus on one person—someone who makes you smile. He had scanned the people crowded along the sidewalk until he came to Louise's frail figure and the stunning brunette next to her.

Something about the woman was familiar, but Frank couldn't place her. If she was one of Louise's friends from school, the last time he might have seen her she would still have been in a school dress and braids. Regardless of who she was, though, she embodied beauty. Frank couldn't have torn his eyes from her if he had tried. And when she chased after Louise's silly dog…he smiled. He only switched his attention to someone else when he could no longer see her. Wallace Tuttle, a man a few years ahead of him in school, stood in front of the general store with his new wife and a little boy in short pants. Married and settled down. What Frank's folks wanted for him, although they never came out and said so.

The face of the lovely brunette flashed before his eyes again as he entered the changing room, and he shook his head in an effort to clear away the vision.

He removed the heavy coat, leaving a lightweight vest and blousy cotton shirt to cover his chest. If only the wind would blow, he could stay cooler. He tugged a comb through his hair, flattening the spot that always wanted to curl over his forehead.

"Come on out. You can't hide away forever." Louise's girlish voice called to him from outside the door. "Your adoring public awaits you."

He growled softly, but Louise must have heard. "I'm kidding. It's just me and my friend."

Her friend—the woman he had so admired along the parade route? He slicked down his hair one final time, laughed at himself for worrying about his looks and left the room.

Seen up close, the woman was even prettier than she had appeared from his vantage point on the wagon. A simple red cotton dress with white buttons highlighted the youthful bloom in her cheeks. Her short, almost black hair waved away from her face. Amber sparkled in the depths of eyes as dark as coal.

"We're so glad you're home." The beauty's voice was a lilting soprano, pleasant to the ear. "Louise has been talking about nothing else for weeks, and I know Preston is eager to see you again."

Preston Nash. Frank sorted mentally through the frequent correspondence he'd had with his former teacher. "You must be Winifred Tuttle."

"Don't sound so surprised." Her laughter tickled his ears. "And please call me Winnie. Everybody else does."

"Little Winnie. The last time I saw you…" He stopped as a picture formed in his mind. He doubted the delicate young woman in front of him would want to be reminded of the occasion.

"I was knee deep in mud, wrestling with my nephews over a fish." She laughed with unselfconscious humor that told him she didn't hang on to any ladylike notions of delicacy.

Frank grinned at the memory. "Do you still like to fish?"

"All the time," Winnie said. "That's still my favorite fishing hole."

Louise said, "Now that you're home, Frank, you'll have to go with her sometime."

Frank started to protest. Home less than twenty-four hours and already his sister was setting him up with a date? He looked into Winnie's laughing dark eyes, the amber glints suggesting both humor and embarrassment, and the prospect of spending more time with his sister's friend appealed to him greatly. "I'd like that."

"I'll try to stay out of the mud this time." Winnie flashed a smile at him, one that revealed teeth with a hint of a space between the two top incisors. Endearing. "But we've kept you long enough. The whole town of Maple Notch—all of Chittenden County, for that matter—can't wait to welcome their hero."

The joy Frank had felt in the banter slid away. "That was a long time ago." His voice fell flat, and he offered an apologetic smile. "It's not so important in the big scheme of things."

"Nonsense. We never had a chance to celebrate your win at Nationals properly." Louise wouldn't let it go.

No, because my accident put an end to all that. I finally figured out I would never skate in competition again.

"Not so long ago. We have long memories around these parts." Winnie spoke softly, but her eyes said more than her tongue.

Don't let her shining eyes beguile you. She's only another fan who adores you for what you used to be. Not what you've become.

A has-been.

Chapter 2

Winnie watched Frank's broad back as he worked his way through the throng of well-wishers, away from her. Here was her chance to ask him her question, and what did she talk about? The old fishing hole, of all things. She wanted to spend time with her hero, the best skater Vermont had ever produced, but not by the creek bed.

Calling herself every kind of fool, Winnie felt rather than heard someone come up beside her. She knew who it was before his deep, gravelly voice confirmed it.

"Happy Fourth of July, Winnie." Preston Nash had first created an ice rink in Maple Notch so Frank could practice year round and coached him through early competitions.

"Hello, Preston. Did you enjoy the parade?" Winnie turned in time to see the older man's mouth curve in a crooked smile. "I expected to see you on the float with Frank. Mr. Sawtelle, I mean." What should she call him? How should one refer to a man she had known since before her parents died when she was a little girl?

"I wanted to let Frank have his moment in the sun. The Lord knows he earned it. Didn't need me taggin' along. I'll see him later, right enough."

They both stared after Frank's retreating figure, Winnie continuing to silently scold herself for thinking such nonsense. To see him walk, his straight carriage and proud bearing, she would never guess he had sustained a career-ending injury. Both ankles shattered, she had heard. Winnie knew better than most how delicate the tendons and bones were that made intricate skating moves possible. How sad.

"Did you ask him?" Preston broke the silence.

Winnie shook her head in answer. "I didn't get a chance."

Preston tugged at a tuft of beard. "I'll see you Monday mornin', then. Usual time."

"Right after my morning chores." Winnie couldn't stop skating any more than she could stop breathing.

Pushed by habits ingrained from childhood, Frank arose before dawn on Monday, milked the cows and slipped his skates over his shoulder before heading to the old mill. For as long he could remember, he had headed to the mill pond every day. Nash—Mr. Nash as he'd called him at the time—had always welcomed him and never minded the presence of the young farm boy around the heavy machinery. That was before he converted the building to a year-round rink.

As Frank started out, he marveled at the dedication of his younger self. How much longer the two miles must have seemed for his short legs. He ran everywhere in those days, loping ahead of his dog, Cotter. Good ol' Cotter, who gave up the ghost about the time Frank's dreams did.

As if he had conjured up a dog, he heard a yipping

sound. Toodles was all girl, impossibly white and fluffy. "Go away. You caused enough mischief yesterday."

Toodles ran around in a circle, sat down and stared at Frank with a yip.

"Stupid dog." In Louise's absence, he didn't have to be polite to the pygmy dog. "Go home."

Toodles angled her ear in his direction, tongue hanging out.

"I don't have anything for you." Bending over, he buried his hand in her silky hair and sighed. "If you insist. Louise won't like you deserting her for me." He started walking again and Toodles trotted beside him, her little feet moving double time to keep up with him. "Then again, maybe she sent you after me." He looked down at the hairy snowball. "Come on. We've got a ways to go."

Before long, the old mill came into view. Nowadays people took their wheat and corn to a mechanized mill in Burlington to be ground into flour. The mill had gone the way of so much else in the country, heavy equipment replacing hard labor and squeezing out small farmers by the thousands since Black Tuesday back in 1929.

But Nash had made the change long before that, using the Glaciarium built in London in 1876 as his model. He'd poured a concrete floor and added earth, cow hair and wooden planks. Over that he had laid copper pipes and then poured water on top. He experimented with the right gasses to pump through the pipes until he found the best mixture for easy, low-cost year-round maintenance.

Frank had had a brief conversation with Nash at the town picnic, arranging for an early practice time this morning. Maybe Frank would have a chance to soak up some of his old mentor's peace and wisdom. He had left Maple Notch poised on the edge of greatness and had returned a failure, at least in his own eyes.

Frank wondered if the door to the mill opened with the

same squeak that gave him away when he was a youngster. Back then, he came to the rink to be alone. On the ice he could control his surroundings, think undisturbed. Nash always knew when he was there, and would make his way down the stairs from his apartment overhead with a bite to eat. Today, smoke curled from the chimney in welcome, even though the morning air felt sticky with heat already.

The door creaked, and Frank stepped into the darkened rink, letting his eyes adjust before flicking the light switch. Itching to start, he sat down on a bench by the door.

Light spilled across the ice from the lantern-lit recesses of Nash's office. "Frank! I was expecting you. Come on in, I put the coffee on."

Toodles dashed in the direction of the friendly voice, but her feet slid from underneath her.

"Don't say I didn't warn you." Pup in his arms, Frank walked across the slippery ice as if it was dry ground.

"Who's this?" Nash scratched the dog under her chin, and she wiggled with pleasure.

"Toodles. Don't laugh. She's Louise's dog."

Nash cocked an eyebrow. "Don't have to explain nuthin' to me." He reached for the coffeepot on top of the stove. "Want anythin' in your coffee?" He poured liquid as black as oil and probably about as thick into the cup.

"What do you have?" Frank played along. It was an old joke between them. Nash's cupboard was as bare as a corn patch in wintertime.

"I know what you're thinkin'." Nash shook his finger at Frank. "Right this moment, I have cream and suguh and cocoa powduh."

"All the makings for hot chocolate." Frank was impressed. "I'll have my coffee black, if it's all the same to you."

"Kids today, they all want sumthin' more than ice when they come."

Frank held back a chuckle. Nash would do anything for kids. He drained the coffee in one long gulp, the only way to drink the irredeemable sludge, and set the mug down. "That was good. Got my blood stirring."

"So're you back for good?"

Frank sensed this was the question Nash had wanted to ask all along. He shrugged. "Might as well. It's not like I was accomplishing much elsewhere."

"A man can do a lot of good here in Maple Notch." Nash paused. "I did. Found you, didn't I?"

Frank chuckled. Nash didn't go in for false modesty. "Maybe we found each other."

"I like to think God brought us together at the right time." Nash set down his mug. "The ice is free. Go on out and warm up. 'Spect you've got some thinkin' to do."

Nash knows me too well. Frank removed his shoes and tied on his skates. Good and snug, so tight he felt as though his foot couldn't breathe. Just the way Nash had tightened his laces the first time. "Your ankles need all the support they can git," the old man had said. More true now than ever.

Frank took a few steps to the edge of the ice, put his hands behind his back in his old habit and pushed off. Lead with the right leg, one long smooth glide, then to the left. A slow, lazy motion that left time suspended in midair. No one to impress here. No need for tricks or jumps or fancy footwork. Just him and the ice that felt more natural under his feet than hard earth.

A tune sprang to Frank's lips. *Encamped along the hills of light...*

He moved in time with the music. His glides grew shorter, faster, as the music sped up and down, his heart pounding in anticipation of the next swell. When he reached the high point of "oh, glorious victory," he jumped into the air, his whole body twirling, and landed on one foot, the other flung out behind him. And he scores a perfect six! In his memory he heard the roar of the crowd.

A solitary figure waiting at the edge of the rink clapped.

Winnie watched Frank in awe. His movements flowed, as graceful, as powerful as ever. She sensed he wanted to be alone, but when he executed the perfect axel, her hands came together of their own accord.

He dug his toes into the ice and stopped, staring in her direction. "Winnie? Is that you?"

Heat spread across her cheeks, heat that had nothing to do with the July weather pounding down outside the building. Inside the rink, she was comfortable, at least until she started skating.

"I didn't mean to interrupt. But this is my normal time to skate and…" *And Preston specifically asked me to show up this morning.*

"It's not my ice. Come on." He turned his back to her and effortlessly skated in dizzying circles to the far end of the ice.

Winnie sat on the bench and laced up her skates, dallying in her nervousness. She hadn't felt this self-conscious about getting on the ice since her first competition, a local winter carnival when she was but seven years old. Frank had skated as well, she remembered, already an accomplished competitor at the ripe old age of twelve, beating all the adults by a mile or more. He was clearly destined for great things.

And he'd come by and said, "Well done, squirt." Maybe that's when her hero worship of Frank Sawtelle had started. With a kind word from an adolescent boy.

But she wasn't seven anymore and he wasn't twelve, competing at the same local festival. He was a national champion, and she was still an untested commodity.

Frank glanced over his shoulder and smiled that same

smile that had dazzled her as a girl. "What's keeping you, squirt?"

Winnie's skates slid onto the ice. She was drawn toward him as if his words were magnets pulling the steel of her blades in his direction. She forced herself to stand still, determined not to succumb to the siren song of his effortless skating. The ice in this rink was more than big enough for both of them. She headed in the opposite direction and went into a spin.

Today she had determined to work on her figure eights. Basic footwork, so boring, but so necessary if she was ever to win at competition. She dug the toe of her right skate into the ice, mentally marking the point where her lines should cross after each loop. She skated forward at a right angle, turned and then returned at a left angle, crossed the center point and repeated the process below.

She studied the faint lines of the school figures her skates had made on the ice. Fair, but not good. Her loops were lopsided. Again. Ten tries later, she was satisfied with her form. Now she sought to run her blades along the same groove as the perfect figure. Six times, a dozen. She turned around, ready to repeat the process backward, and glanced up into Frank's face only a few feet away.

"That's tedious work." Nothing more than that.

"I'm not very good at it." She made a face. If she wanted to impress Frank, this wasn't the way. Not doing compulsory figures. Foolish, Winnie. Why didn't you practice toe loops instead?

"You're doing fine. But would you like to take a break and do something different? I—" Here his voice broke a little, and he cleared his throat. "I like skating with a partner once in a while."

Winnie couldn't remember saying anything. It was a wonder she didn't collapse at Frank's feet. *He's asking me to skate with him?* Her dreams soared to the clouds and her feet turned to lead. Nevertheless, she must have done something to indicate agreement, because he had grasped her hands in his and pulled her beside him.

Skating together. With Frank Sawtelle.

Chapter 3

Frank's arm circled Winnie's waist, pulling her close to him as they worked on matching their steps. He shortened his long strides to her shorter ones, she lengthened hers, and soon they moved together in unison. The slight pressure of his arm on the small of her back sent her nerves on a thrill ride. He took her hand in his and skated backwards in a variation of a polka. No wonder some church folk frowned on dancing, if it made her feel like this. No one in the world existed except for the man at her side, touching her here, there, guiding their bodies as one in time to the music.

Under Frank's gentle tutelage, Winnie relaxed, and her steps flowed in time to inaudible music. After this, maybe she could do the figure eights with more ease. She imagined them as a kind of waltz, three steps in a triangular circle.

"You've got it." Frank's voice was as melodious as the music singing through her veins. He dropped his hands, but the connection between them stayed, strengthened.

He skated backward and she did, too, the two of them continuing to match steps, forming a perfect line of body and leg and arms.

Frank spoke from time to time, his voice echoing her thoughts. "Watch your toe there. Lift higher. Careful with the corners." Before long, he made a circle with his fingers, an indication that he wanted to jump. She saw his mouth form the words, "One…two…three…!" Together they leaped into the air in perfect harmony, toes landing back on the ice at the same moment. Winnie smiled in triumph. Never had she skated so well.

Frank didn't fare as well, overbalancing and landing on the ice.

"Are you hurt?" Winnie chastised herself for forgetting his injury. He didn't have any obvious weakness to remind her.

He stood and brushed ice shavings from his trouser legs. "Just my pride." He pushed off in a slide, shaking his arms and legs as if in a last effort to get rid of the tingles in his side. "Don't worry about me. I won't do anything out here to endanger the use of my legs. Gotta be of some use about the farm."

Winnie held her tongue. Men didn't like to be fussed over. They retreated to opposite sides of the rink, unlaced their skates and prepared to return outside. Winnie glanced over the barrier and saw Frank petting Louise's dog. A shaft of light pierced the dark rink when he opened the door. Toodles ran around him in circles, barking at the prospect of the walk home. Frank turned to wave goodbye, his face framed in a halo of sunshine. "See you later, squirt."

The joy returned to Winnie's soul.

A week later, Toodles was already waiting by the screen door when Frank left. "If I don't take you, you'll wake up the whole house, is that it? Well, come on then." He opened the door, and the little dog wiggled through. "Don't think you can make a habit of this, mind you. You're supposed to be Louise's dog."

Toodles looked at him with a question in her eyes.

"Oh, I know, she doesn't get up so early these days. So what? You can wait until a little later, can't you?"

A series of yips ended in a screech that would have done a crow credit. Make that a rooster. Toodles was definitely an up-with-the-dawn kind of dog.

Dew had fallen overnight, and wet grass brushed the hems of Frank's trousers. Toodles bounded through the growth, stopping every now and then to check out an interesting scent. Frank whistled a few stray notes of "Faith Is the Victory." Well, why not? He had felt more secure on the ice yesterday than he had in months. As dark and old-fashioned as Nash's rink was, it remained his first and best venue.

Encamped along the hills of light. Frank lifted his gaze to the mountains surrounding him. He had missed the sight during his years away in Boston and New York. Nothing could replace the green hills of home. Today, with early morning sunshine breaking over and between the mountaintops, they looked like hills of light indeed. Was he one of the soldiers mentioned in the song? Not hardly. If faith was the victory, then his faith had failed the test when it came to the crucial moment.

Stop thinking like that. Now he faced a new battle in a new arena. Today, walking through the hills of light, he could almost believe things would turn out better in this fight. That Louise would get better and that Dad would figure out a way to keep the farm.

And that…this morning…he might run into the beautiful Winnie Tuttle again.

The old mill appeared in the distance, and Frank sped up his steps.

* * *

Winnie hurried through her chores in order to take an extra few minutes in the family bathroom.

"Winnie, will you hurry up in there?" Clarinda, Winnie's older sister, pleaded. Winnie knew she shouldn't dawdle. Clarinda was expecting for the fifth time, and this time was harder than the first four. Even with the early days of pregnancy behind her, she stayed sick to her stomach and needed the restroom first thing every morning. If only this wasn't the only decent mirror in the house....

"Just a minute." Winnie sighed at her unruly hair that refused to stay in careful curls, pulled back her bangs with a metal clasp and straightened the collar on her blouse.

She didn't want to primp too much or else the questions would start. She opened the door to see Clarinda bent over at the waist, clutching her sides as if that would hold in the sickness. She bolted past Winnie and a moment later was sick to her stomach.

"Oh, Clarinda, I'm so sorry." Winnie grabbed a washcloth, dampened it and then held it to her sister's forehead until she stopped coughing up what little breakfast she had managed to eat. "Do you need to see the doctor?"

Clarinda lifted her wan face, framed by dark hair sprinkled with gray. She struggled to her feet. "Don't need a doctor. It's just the baby. I'll be fine." She took in Winnie's careful grooming. "I got your blouse dirty. I'm so sorry."

"I'm fine," Winnie lied. She had worn her favorite blouse on purpose; bright yellow looked good with her dark hair. At least, that's what Louise said, when she wasn't busy teasing her. "I'll wash it out and it'll be as good as new." But not now. She'd put it to soak and...stop wanting to rush away. So often, the needs of her family and her own desire to get to the ice squeezed Winnie in a vicious vise.

Setting her mind to the task at hand, she stayed by the

bathroom door until she was sure Clarinda wouldn't get sick again. When she heard the tap running, she scuttled away and put on the first blouse that came to hand, white with pink trim and rose-petal buttons. A little girl's blouse. That's probably how Frank saw her, if he thought of her at all.

By the time Winnie finished, Clarinda had returned to the kitchen, humming to herself as if she had never been sick a day in her life. Only the paleness of her cheeks suggested anything amiss.

"Should I expect you home at the usual time? After lunch?" Clarinda looked up from where she was chopping apples.

"If it's not too much trouble." Winnie gave her usual response and held her breath. So far, Clarinda was holding up, in spite of the difficult pregnancy. But what about the time when her pregnancy advanced, and Winnie had to give up skating, or her volunteer work at the soup kitchen, or both, to help more around the house? What if her sister-in-law, Mary Anne, needed help, as well?

"I'm fine. I appreciate your staying late this morning. Now get going." Clarinda shooed her away with her usual smile.

The Tuttles' dog, a gangly mutt named Rover, barked a greeting as Winnie headed out the door. Her niece Betty jumped up from where she squatted by the animal. "Hi, Auntie Winnie! Can I skate with you today?"

Betty asked almost every day, even though her father had said no. From his perspective, one person in the family with her head in the clouds was enough. The farm had provided for the Tuttle family since before the Revolutionary War, and he expected his children to continue the tradition.

"You know what your father says. Not until it gets cold enough for the pond to freeze on its own."

At last Winnie was free of the house and moved at a

ladylike pace until she left the yard. As she passed the boundary stone, she allowed herself a single skip. Although Winnie treasured her niece, she wouldn't have welcomed her company this morning. She hoped Frank would be there again, that they would have another chance to skate together. She wanted to recapture last week's magic.

When she arrived at the old mill and opened the door, a tall figure emerged from the shadows. "Good morning, Winnie."

She thought she saw a hint of a smile on his face. "Good morning, Frank." She perched on the bench to slip on her skates and then joined him on the ice.

She skated a few warm-up laps. Strange that no matter how busy she stayed on the farm, the ice required a different set of muscles. She worked the compulsory figures, no longer worried that Frank might see or criticize. Would he invite her to partner with him again? She shook her head. She shouldn't hope too much.

A few moments later, an arm slipped around her waist. Long legs encased in sturdy blue denim glided in time with hers. She relaxed. This part of the dream, at least, was real. As they skated together, she felt sheltered, secure in the knowledge he would never let her fall. After a while, they separated but continued skating with no more than a foot between them.

When they rose together in the axel jump, Winnie crashed. Frank extended his arm to help her stand. "My fault. I got us into the turn too soon."

Embarrassment flooded her body and into her cheeks. "Thank you, but I think I missed that all on my own. I have trouble with that particular jump."

Frank cocked an eyebrow. "I wouldn't have guessed. You seem very comfortable on the ice. Let me see you jump."

The ease Winnie had felt in their partnership dwindled

into nothingness, and a tremor passed down her legs. *It's nothing you haven't done a thousand times before,* she reminded herself. But never with a former national champion watching. "I don't know."

"Do it." His tone left no room for argument. He skated away, giving her plenty of room to move.

Winnie took a deep breath, glanced behind her and began rapid strokes of her skates. She reached optimum speed, lifted her skates in the air, twisted her body…and landed on one foot, then both, before crashing to the ice.

"Again. Keep your body straight this time."

Winnie's shins stung where they had contacted the ice. Her dungarees would show wear and tear, and Clarinda would complain about the waste. Nevertheless, Winnie gritted her teeth, pushed herself to her feet and took off again. This time she straightened…overcompensated… fell worse than the last time.

"Again. Find the happy medium."

Where had her pleasant skating companion of the morning gone? She would have matching bruises on both shins come tomorrow morning, and would have a hard time skating at all. Working with Frank Sawtelle no longer seemed like such a good idea.

She stood, skating a few circles to get her legs back under her.

"Now!" Toodles might have barked the words, so fierce was Frank's command. Winnie grimaced, but increased her rhythm, rose in the air…and landed perfectly.

"Again." Frank's voice commanded.

Winnie had had enough. One glance at the clock told her it was past time for her to get to town or else brunch would be late for the church's soup kitchen visitors. "I can't. I have to go." She skated to the edge of the rink, changed into her street shoes and left, all the while waiting for the silent figure to say one word of praise.

His silence followed her out the door.

Chapter 4

"Where are you headed with Toodles today?" Louise stuck her head out of her bedroom window, on the ground floor now that she found the stairs difficult. The little dog barked happily at the sight of her mistress, jumping up and landing her nails on the windowsill as if encouraging her to come out and join the fun.

"Keep yelling like that, and you'll wake up the house." Guilt assailed Frank and he joined Louise at the window. "Are you all right?"

"I'm fine." Louise waved away his concern, although the sister he used to know would have climbed out of the window and walked with him to the ice rink. "You've been going to the mill pretty regularly. Something special going on that a sister should know about?"

Nothing except Louise's best friend. "No. I didn't quit skating, just competition. I still feel more at home on the ice than anywhere else." Shattered ankles hadn't broken a lifetime habit.

Louise cocked her head, studying him. "There's more to it than that. I know that Winnie skates every morning. She'd even go on Sunday if she thought she could get away with it." She grinned. "Like you."

Frank didn't dare admit that he had come to enjoy those early morning sessions, especially not to his romance-minded sister. "I'd better go before it gets much later. If you're sure you're all right."

"Go on ahead."

Toodles made another attempt to jump through the window. When she didn't succeed, she cast a woeful look in Louise's direction and trotted after Frank. When he waved goodbye, Louise said, "Say hi to Winnie for me."

Nodding, he jogged down the path. The exercise cleared his mind as he shifted gears from home to the ice. More and more, Winnie filled his thoughts. Anyone who kept going after some of the falls she'd taken this week…falls he had pushed on her with his demands…was serious about her sport. If she didn't realize how good she was, Nash must. Frank held no illusions as to the reason his old mentor wanted them on the ice at the same time. The only question was when, not if, they asked for his help in preparing Winnie for competition.

Frank had sworn to leave that world behind. He didn't want to become one of those skaters who faded into the background as coaches, living on in the shadow of someone else's dreams. Some people argued that he was obligated to share his knowledge and experience, but he had said a firm "no." His decision had never wavered until he saw Winnie Tuttle on the ice less than two weeks ago. It seemed like an eternity.

Nash had told him Winnie worked with the youngest skaters, those too young for school. Some people thought Vermonters were born with skates on their feet, but few of them developed much beyond a pleasant afternoon's exercise. With the Depression, few people paid for the use of the year-round ice. If Frank could help Nash promote his rink by offering lessons, he should.

When Frank entered the mill, only dim lights lit the interior, not the bright bulbs in use when someone was on the ice. Toodles stepped to the edge of the ice and stopped. Her frequent forays onto the slippery surface had discouraged her from racing ahead. Instead, she ran along the boards that circled the ice, yipping as if asking why he wasn't skating yet.

Light poured from Nash's office overhead, and Frank could see Winnie's dark hair bobbing up and down behind the window. He grinned at the sight. She could get as excited as a child. He already knew her favorite poet—Robert Frost, of course! He lived in Vermont after all—her favorite book (*Pride and Prejudice*) and a host of other useless information. Her sentences tended to come out sounding like exclamations. She provided a good antidote to the dreariness of life at home.

When he headed upstairs, she waited at the door to the office. "Preston has coffee for us today."

Nash always had a pot on the stove, even on the hottest days of summer. Maybe all that coffee explained Winnie's exuberance. He accepted the mug from her hand. Her mug was identified with her name carved into the side, perhaps a memento from a family trip before the Depression put a stop to such frivolity.

"Come in and take a load off your feet." Nash had turned the phrase into a joke after he had explained that a skater had to take good care of his feet and ankles because they were his lifelines on the ice.

Toodles barked and placed her two front paws on Winnie's lap. She fed the dog a bit of a doughnut, then another, until Toodles finished most of Winnie's breakfast.

"You really shouldn't give her that, you know. She's

plenty fat enough." Frank whistled the dog over and gave her a tiny bite.

Winnie chuckled. "Oh, I know, but she's just so cute when she begs." Toodles nosed around the floor for a final crumb. Winnie turned her attention to Nash.

So now they would have the conversation Frank was expecting. Over and over again he had asked God's opinion since it first occurred to him last week, but he still wasn't sure.

Nash uncrossed his legs and settled his feet on the floor. "Winnie here won both the Vermont championship and the all–New England competition last year. She placed within shouting distance of getting a medal at Nationals."

Two bright red spots appeared on Winnie's cheeks.

"Senior level?" Frank asked. Some girls switched when they were only sixteen. A year ago Winnie would have been, what, seventeen?

She nodded, the blush spreading down her neck. Frank decided to ease her embarrassment. "Well done."

Heat scalded Winnie from her hairline to her shoulders at Frank's simple compliment. This man epitomized championship skating. Compared to him, she was an amateur. He could help her to reach her goals.

With a brief prayer for courage, a repetition of the same prayer she had repeated every day for the past week, she leaned forward. "Frank, next year I want to win Nationals, and God willing, I want to go further." There, she had said it, putting her greatest dreams into words. "And I'd like you to help me."

He rubbed his jaw line. "Nationals are less than a year away, a little over six months. That's not much time." He stared at the floor a long time.

Toodles jumped into Winnie's lap, as if sensing her worry, and nuzzled the crook of her arm.

Winnie fought the squirms that made her want to tap her foot. She was foolish, thinking that a champion like Frank Sawtelle…

"It'll mean a lot of hard work. You're good, you're very good." He looked up just long enough for her to see a fleeting smile, and her insides quivered in anticipation. "But there are a lot of talented women out there." Frank looked back at the floor before he continued speaking. "Early mornings, even earlier than we've been coming. Maybe some evenings, too, after the day's work is done." He looked up. "But I'm willing to give it a try. Although this man here taught me everything I know. Maybe you should ask *him* to help out."

Preston's laughter filled the room, almost rattling the mug she held in her hands. Setting it on the edge of his desk, she clapped. "You don't know how much this means to me. I'll work as hard as it takes."

She opened her mouth to say more, but Frank raised a finger to his lips. "Don't make me regret it before we even start." He stood. "Let's get down to the ice."

"Now?"

"Yes, now. We can't waste a minute." He left the room and headed down the stairs as if he hadn't just given her dreams wrapped in gold.

"Well, what are you waiting for? Go on down to the ice and get started." Preston shooed her out of the office.

Winnie looked back at the bent head of the man who meant so much to her…and ahead to the man who represented her future. Solomon's words from Ecclesiastes, about a threefold cord, came to her mind. Past, present, future—together, the three of them might repeat Maple Notch's supremacy in the ice-skating world.

By the end of the session, Winnie's hopes lay flat on the ice. Frank had done nothing but review basic skating techniques. Skating forward, skating backward, gathering speed…no compulsory figures. No jumps. Just first year, first week, skating basics. How could she prepare for international-level competition at this pace?

Frank called an abrupt halt to their practice session. "Come here an hour earlier on Monday. We'll discuss our schedule after that."

While Winnie changed to her shoes, Frank continued skating. He jumped a couple of times, easily executing doubles, like a bird stretching its wings after being earthbound for too long. As he came off the ice, he was whistling the chorus to "Faith Is the Victory," his signature song.

Winnie smiled. "I'll be here on Monday morning." She headed for the exit. If she headed cross country, she should get to the soup kitchen in time to help fix the noon meal.

Mosquitos feasted on her exposed arms, making her wish she had worn a long-sleeved shirt. Footsteps pounded behind her, and she turned around to see Frank following her. "You're not heading home."

She shook her head but didn't elaborate. "How has Louise been this week?"

"About the same." Frank didn't expand on that. "Nobody will tell me much, they just asked me to come home. I knew it must be serious."

Winnie nodded. That was what she had suspected. Everyone thought he had left Maple Notch for good, like a lot of young people had over the past decade.

"Do you go to the same place every day, after practice? You're always walking away from your house."

His question made Winnie a little uneasy. She wasn't ashamed of what she did in town, far from it, but she didn't like to brag about it either. What if… "How about you come with me and see? You might find it…enlightening."

His eyes narrowed, and she felt compelled to explain. "I help out at a soup kitchen at the church in the mornings.

Maple Notch is better off than some of the bigger cities, but plenty of people around here are hurting."

He grimaced. "I wish I could come with you, but my family is expecting me home and I have to earn my bread and butter. Maybe another time?" His lips curled. "What if I ask you to give up your benevolence ministry for skating?"

Winnie kept her voice level as she said, "I pray it won't come to that. Maybe you can come another time." She sped up, changing direction, before she broke down crying. Why did she feel like God pulled her in ten directions at once? How could one person help her sister with the children, help the hungry of the community and spend hours a day skating, all at the same time?

Was Winnie selfish to want a gold medal?

Chapter 5

Frank sat in the Sawtelle family pew, between his father and Louise. Coming back to the Maple Notch Community Church was as much a homecoming as his mother's cooking and the cool stillness of the ice rink. Its four walls had heard his prayer for salvation, and its people were as close as family.

Pastor Rucker asked the congregation to turn to the second chapter of James, verse fourteen. "If a brother or sister be naked, and destitute of daily food."

The words arrested Frank's attention. Those words had new meaning in 1931, ones he'd only glimpsed as a child. For some reason, he had hoped Maple Notch had escaped the financial malaise that had befallen the country. But Winnie had indicated some of the locals needed the services of a food kitchen.

Winnie sat across the aisle. In some ways, she was as bubbly as any fan he had encountered. In other ways, she was a warm, vibrant, very real woman. Her smile reflected inner joy more than a carefree life. She worked hard when skating and spent the noon hour at a soup kitchen before heading home to a houseful of her sister's children. New England born and raised, she was ready to face adversity, like most of the folks around Maple Notch.

In fact, she was the kind of woman Frank dreamed of marrying someday.

He shook his head to rid himself of such thoughts. As long as he was Winnie's coach, there was no room for any romantic folderol from either one of them. As far as he knew, she didn't have a boyfriend. Good. Her dream allowed no room for distractions.

Frank forced his attention back to the sermon. The pastor was reminding them that faith and works went hand in hand. Frank's faith in himself had fallen short of his goal—the gold in 1928. Had he allowed his dedication to stray too far from God?

After the final amen, Frank helped Louise out of the pew. She asked, "Are you coming to the youth meeting tonight?"

Youth? He supposed that at twenty-three he still qualified, but he felt ages older than the young people fresh out of high school, like Louise—or Winnie. "Is there anyone my age that comes?"

"A few confirmed bachelors and spinsters and some recent college grads." She followed the direction of his gaze. "Winnie and I are the newcomers to the group. Excuse me, I want to say hi to her. I haven't seen her this week."

People parted as Louise approached them, making room for her to pass. Even with the sturdy cane, she shuffled more than walked, but her smile remained as bright as ever. Every few steps, people stopped her for hugs, greetings, conversation. She was a treasured part of the community.

Before Louise reached Winnie, someone tapped Frank on the shoulder. Turning, he encountered Bob Richardson, a friend from high school. "Hey, Sawtelle, welcome home. You know Kay, of course." His wife, a petite blonde Frank recognized, shyly waved.

Two children clung to Bob's knees and he held a baby in his arms, a charming boy who smiled and waved his arms. Frank accepted the baby's invitation, taking him in his arms and rubbing noses. Family. A part of life Frank had yet to enjoy.

They exchanged pleasantries, but Frank suspected they wouldn't see much of each other. Glancing around the sanctuary, he only spotted one other unmarried man his age, and no single women past the age of twenty. When he had gone from Maple Notch, he had left more than family behind. People he had known all his life no longer saw him as a friend, but as some idol risen far above his humble roots. Better than anyone, he knew how quickly gold tarnished. He didn't belong anywhere anymore.

"Frank!" Someone touched his shoulder. Turning, he found Winnie behind him. Her older sister Clarinda waited beside her. "Oh, excuse me, Bob." She smiled her apologies at the school friend.

"We'll catch up later," Bob said.

Clarinda extended a hand for a welcome shake. "I understand my sister didn't pass along my invitation to join us for dinner today."

Before Frank could answer, Winnie frowned, and Frank wondered if she disliked the idea. She must have noticed his concern. "It's only that I don't want to make any more demands on your time than I already have."

"Nonsense." Clarinda sounded as practical as ever, a picture of her headmistress aunt in the making. "It's selfish to keep him to yourself. The rest of us want to visit our old friend."

Wallace Tuttle extended his hand in greeting. "Please

say you'll come. Clarinda will give us no peace, otherwise. Your whole family is invited, if they wish to come."

Winnie laughed. "Louise comes over most Sundays, if I'm not at your house. We've given you a couple of weeks' break, figuring you'd like to visit together before the whole community descended on your doorstep."

Unlike their daily practice sessions? Frank decided to accept the invitation before they gave him more reasons. "I would love to join you, if Mom and Dad are agreeable."

The family climbed into the back of the Tuttles' battered pickup truck. "Ride with us, Mr. Sawtelle." Howard and Clarinda's oldest boy motioned for him to climb into the back of the truck.

"Go ahead," Dad said. Frank climbed in and sat across from Winnie and next to the oldest Finch boy, and soon they rattled down the road.

Tuttle Bridge approached. He missed the Old Bridge, and the way wooden wagon wheels trundled over the planks and in the shadows caused by the barnlike structure. But the structure had washed away three-and-a-half years before, in the flood of 1927. He hadn't seen the new bridge until he had returned home last week. Double-wide, still covered with a red roof, it lacked the romantic appeal of the original bridge, in spite of the new courting board tacked to the entrance.

His eyes wandered to Winnie, who sat across from him on a bale of hay, talking in Louise's ear. Times like this, she reminded him of the schoolgirl she had been when he left Maple Notch. Her ready smile made her a great performer on the ice, as long as she wasn't concentrating on her steps, that is. That same smile probably brightened the day for everyone who came to the soup kitchen.

"Why doesn't President Hoover do something?" Winnie's voice rose above the clamor of the children.

Louise shrugged. Frank leaned forward and raised his

voice to be heard. "That's the question of the year, isn't it?" Did he dare bring up some of the things Hoover had done right, at least from Frank's perspective? "He did warn us that the collapse was coming, but nobody listened."

Winnie gave him a look that could have withered a cow's udder. "But isn't that the president's job? To make people listen and do what's best for the country?"

"That's enough!" Louise scolded. "Don't get Winnie started, Frank. She'll talk your ear off. She won every debate last year at the Seminary."

A dark pink suffused Winnie's cheeks, but she sat back against the side of the truck. "I'm sorry. I let my mouth get ahead of me." She smiled. "If you ever want to get me mad on the ice, all you have to say is 'Herbert Hoover.'"

Frank nodded. "I'll keep that in mind." So politics captured Winnie's interest, not that the fact surprised him. He should have expected it; her great-grandmother Clara Tuttle's picture hung in the library because of her leadership in women's education and the suffrage movement, in Vermont and beyond.

Winnie was dressed in a pleasant plaid dress with a blue, navy and gray pattern. The collar ended with a tie at the bottom of the V-neck, and a thin blue belt lay snug around a dropped waist. The wind blew her curly dark hair into a frothy mess that suited her animated face.

Smart, pretty, concerned, generous—and one of the best skaters Frank had ever seen.

In earlier times, Clarinda would have cooked two chickens to feed a group this size. Today she chose the biggest hen in the yard and added extra deviled eggs and mashed potatoes with plenteous gravy.

But no one here would complain. The Sawtelles suffered the same shortages. Louise had confided their family struggles to Winnie. They shared lots of things like that, things both families probably wanted to keep quiet.

Summer heat hadn't helped Louise's pain the way everyone had hoped, but Frank's return brought her such joy that she didn't seem to mind so much. She sat to his right at the table, making sure he got second and third helpings of every dish. She had succumbed to her family's opinion that Frank was too thin.

Winnie disagreed. She had seen him in action on the ice, up close. His body was solid muscle and sinews, lithe and sparse and beautiful. Her face heated at the thoughts flowing through her mind. Frank had everything needed in a skater, until that accident ended his career. Why God would allow that to happen made about as much sense as the financial mess the country was in.

The meal ended, and Winnie headed for the kitchen to help with the dishes after a longing look at their guests headed for the parlor.

"Go ahead out to the living room and enjoy yourself." Clarinda shooed her away. "Look, the boys are coming. The baseball game must be about to start."

"It's a double header today." Clarinda's husband, Howard, stood at the door to the kitchen. "Come on in. The first game has already started."

The boys sat cross-legged in front of the radio. Howard and Mr. Sawtelle sat in rocking chairs, while Frank and Wallace sat on either end of one sofa with the Sawtelle women on the other couch. Winnie slid in between the two men with a sigh of contentment. The Red Sox were doing poorly this season, even with Tom Winsett and Bob Kline batting .333, but none of the pitchers were very good. Their record was 34–57, and today's game against the Detroit Tigers didn't promise much improvement.

"Now, Frank, no offense, but baseball here is a man's sport. It's decided by things anybody can count, like runs and strikes and outs." Howard rubbed his hands together. Baseball was his passion—he had played in college.

Frank didn't even blink an eye. "Some people might disagree with you. Say football is the toughest sport."

Winnie chuckled, and Wallace laughed out loud. "He's got you there, Howard."

Howard joined in the laughter. "Oh, wait. Kline's coming up to bat."

The room remained silent—even Wallace's little boy stayed quiet—as five pitches passed the plate. A hitter's count, it was called, three balls and two strikes.

He struck out, of course. However, the Red Sox went on to a surprise win at 7–6. As the announcers prepared for the second game, Howard turned his attention away from the radio and addressed Frank.

"So, tell me, Frank, why are you encouraging Winnie's fantasies?"

Chapter 6

Frank knew how Winnie felt without looking. He could feel it, in the way her arms tensed where they brushed his, her legs trembling. His fingers dug into the wool of his trousers as he fought for a reasonable response. "It's not a fantasy. She has an excellent chance at placing at Nationals this year, and the Olympics aren't out of the question."

"What?" Clarinda came into the living room from the kitchen. "I know it's a sensitive subject, Frank, but you of all people know how little a gold medal prepares you for the future. A college degree is much more practical, and we can't even afford that. She's the first Tuttle since my grandfather Daniel Jr. not to go to college." She took a seat on the edge of Howard's armchair.

Frank allowed himself to look at Winnie and winced. Her usual smile had disappeared, and her eyes had widened, her irises circles of charred wood against a pale face. If her family objected to her skating, why hadn't they mentioned it before?

Winnie lifted her face, focusing her attention on her brother. "Wallace, you don't agree with them, do you?"

Wallace stared at his hands for a long minute before he looked up. "I was lucky. A publisher paid me to write a book about birds, and then two more. But now the company has closed, and I've had to give up writing. The Olympics are a rich folks' dream. I'm sorry, sis." He looked over Winnie's dark head at Frank. "Things were different when you skated, Frank."

Frank nodded. He knew, only too well. He should have come home as soon as he lost his job, but he had stayed to look for another one. Only Mom's letter about Louise's illness and the family's needing his help on the farm had brought him home at last.

"You're right, of course. But…the international competition represents a dream, a reminder that things will get better. We're fortunate next year. Both competitions will be held in New York state. That's practically next door. And—" Frank glanced at Winnie, at the passion and hope in her eyes "—she's seriously talented."

The smile that lifted her lips made up for a lot of the hurt and misunderstanding fluttering around the room today.

"Talent doesn't put food in the mouth," Howard said.

Clarinda stood before he could speak further. "Let's enjoy our company." She reached for the Radiola. "Isn't it time for the second game to start?" The boys whistled and she turned up the volume.

Mary Anne squeezed into the space between Winnie and Wallace and pressed her sister-in-law's hand. At least one family member offered Winnie support.

The inquisition into Winnie's skating dreams had been postponed—for now. Her family's opposition had given Frank a lot to think about.

* * *

Winnie rose an hour early on Monday. She would have left early even if she hadn't promised to meet Frank for the extra hour's practice. If she stayed, someone might find a reason to keep her home. Yesterday's rejection still hurt, and she didn't feel up to helping Clarinda on this day.

She took the overland route from her house to the mill. After going six days a week since she was twelve, Winnie could find her way and avoid obstacles even if she had a blindfold on. The toe of her shoe scuffed through clods of dirt, and dust coated the worn leather. Her skates were in even worse shape; she had been wearing the same pair since she finished her last growth spurt. Only regular applications of petroleum jelly prevented them from falling apart.

What would Frank say to her? Only two days had passed since he agreed to help her. Would yesterday's confrontation discourage him?

To Winnie's surprise, Preston waited for her at the door. "I thought you might be here early today." A faint smile lifted his lips. "Come on up to my office. We need to talk."

Winnie's heart raced. After yesterday, those words sounded ominous. She forced herself to keep up with Preston's tread on the stairs. He had drilled into her that first impressions mattered, that appearance was two-thirds of competition. She had to look confident, even if she feared she would fall on her first jump. Smile, even if she was angry at the judges' scores. If one day went poorly, come back the next and work harder than ever. She would do her best not to let yesterday's events affect her on the ice.

Her determination fled when the door to Preston's office opened and Frank's figure appeared in the light.

"Thanks for getting here so early. Come on in. I made the coffee today, so it's potable for once."

Accepting her Winnie mug, she perched on the rickety

folding chair Preston kept next to his desk. He had promised the chair was stronger than it looked, like her legs. It would probably fall apart today, just like her spirits.

Keep the smile on your face.

"I'm glad you made it early. I did tell you we needed to start practice an hour earlier, but I didn't know if you could get away?" He lifted the end of the sentence, making it a question.

"I didn't tell them. Yet." Winnie's hands twisted in her lap, until she tucked them under her armpits. "And I wanted to get started. I'm ready." She looked straight at Frank. "If you are."

Frank inhaled. "I know what I want to say, but I want to hear what Nash thinks first." He saluted their mentor with his coffee mug.

Preston pointed his finger at Frank. "I'm not getting in the middle of this one. Seems to me the only one who should be making this decision is Winnie. And you, if you're going to help her."

Frank nodded as if he had expected that response and turned to Winnie. "I want you to think about exactly what you're facing. You already want to do something extraordinary, something very few skaters ever have the chance to do—to compete against the very best skaters in the country, maybe even the world."

Winnie quivered inside. Didn't he think she was good enough? He had said so, but now he was trying to discourage her.

"Think about it. None of the competitions you've ever been in, except Nationals last year, can compare. It's hard. Not everyone can take the pressure."

Winnie sat back against her chair. "I did okay last year."

"That's another thing. You think you're good. You have the potential to be good, maybe even great. But you have no idea what I'm going to put you through these next six

months. You may decide you hate me before we're done."
He allowed himself to smile. "I won't be your friend. I
can't even afford to like you. I have to teach you. I won't
be Louise's brother. I'll be the former national champion
who knows what it takes."

Winnie wanted him to be her coach and nothing more.
Didn't she? Why was she hesitating? "Of course."

He leaned in, close, almost intimate. "What about your
family?"

His question hung in the air, sucking the breath out of
Winnie's lungs, strangling the words in her throat. If she
couldn't explain her heart's desire to these two people,
who else would understand? "When I was younger, I read
a story about Eric Liddell. He's a missionary to China. But
before he went to China, he competed in the Paris Olympics, seven years ago."

As she told the story, the knot loosened in her throat.
"He was the fastest sprinter Scotland had ever seen. His
sister kept telling him he should go to China. That it was
his duty, God's will." She sighed. "Like it's my duty to help
my family and make money if I can." She tapped the floor
with her foot, imagining Liddell pounding the dirt of the
racetrack. "He told his sister that God made him fast. That
he felt God's pleasure when he ran." She looked first at
Preston, then at Frank. "That's the way I feel when I skate."

Preston smiled as if she had given a prize-winning
speech, and Frank just shook his head. "I've heard of Lid-
del. He won the 400-meter race, not a distance a sprinter
normally runs."

"That's my favorite part of the story." Winnie's spirits
lifted. "I know my family doesn't understand, but skating is as essential to me as breathing. I can't stop. I'll give
up sleep. I'll give up food. I could even do the worst thing
my family can imagine—give up books. The only thing I
won't give up is God. And I believe He wants me to skate."

Spirits encouraged by her own pep talk, Winnie stood. "Faith is the victory, after all. I'm ready to skate. How about you?"

Frank's deep chuckle rewarded her. "Let's go, then." Without further discussion, they trotted down the stairs and soon were skating as if they had no other cares in the world.

Frank pushed Winnie through basic moves, repeating them over and over until her legs nearly collapsed from exhaustion. Skating like this was not fun, not at all.

When at last he called an end to the practice, he watched her with hooded eyes as she slowly circled the rink, returning to the gate.

After she put the blade protectors over her skates, she walked to the benches to change into her shoes. "What's wrong? Have you changed your mind?"

"No, I already said you were talented. So talented that you can get by on talent alone at most of the competitions you've gone to," Frank said.

Talent alone? After all the hours she spent practicing?

"But to get to the international level, you have to work hard. Harder than you ever thought possible."

Winnie clamped her jaw shut before she could say something out of turn.

"You're not fast enough into your jumps. You need to strengthen your legs so you can jump higher. Your lines are sloppy." His sentences came out chopped, like those of her physical education instructor at the Seminary, and the expression on his face suggested she should get coal instead of a present in her Christmas stocking.

Winnie looked at Preston, her eyes begging him to speak up for her. Instead, he nodded.

"I told you it would be hard," Frank said. "You just don't know how hard, not yet."

*   *   *

Frank watched Winnie walk away, knowing he had been harsh with her.

"She's tough, you know." Nash waited until she closed the door behind her. "She looks like your younger sister until she gets on the ice."

"Not tough enough. Not yet." Frank tucked his chin against his chest. "But I'll make it my business to get her ready."

"I know." Nash clamped a hand on Frank's shoulder. "I knew I couldn't do anything more for her. She's passed my limitations, pretty much, or maybe I can't be tough enough on a girl who's more like a daughter to me than a pupil."

Frank guffawed. "You had no problems being tough on me."

Nash just gave him a look. "She's going to need both of us, to become everything she can be."

Especially with her family's attitude about her skating. Frank was blessed that he competed when Louise was still in good health and his father was able to work the long, hard hours farming required. But Winnie's family opposed skating for more reasons than the financial hardship. They had ties to Maple Notch back to the beginning and a commitment to education without equal in Vermont. They had a hard time understanding Winnie's pull to a different world.

Friday's practice gave further evidence of their opposition, as if he needed it. After he got to the rink earlier than he had for three days, Winnie arrived five minutes late. When he took her through the first few exercises, her skating looked sloppy, her mind obviously elsewhere.

"What's wrong?"

Frightened eyes flashed at him.

"I won't bite. Maybe I can help."

She shook her head. "Not unless you want to babysit

Wallace's little boy and take care of the house. Mary Anne is, umm, expecting." Her face turned a pretty shade of pink as she said the words. "So is Clarinda, and they are both sicker than they've ever been before. Wallace wants me to move to their house and help Mary Anne out for a few months."

Frank dug his skate into the ice, wanting to duke it out with various members of the Tuttle clan. "Does Clarinda still need your help?"

Winnie shrugged. "I suppose so. She's over getting sick in the mornings, but she gets tired easily. I know you talked about practicing at night, but that's when she needs me most...." Her voice trailed away. "I'm so frustrated I want to scream. And then I feel guilty."

Frank didn't have an answer, but he knew what helped him when he still blamed the world for the accident that ended his skating. "I know what helps me sometimes. Skate around the rink and scream, as loud as you want. Nash and I will understand."

Winnie stared at him as if he were crazy, but then took off. When she was halfway around the rink, a thin sound crept across the ice. As it gained in volume, her skates moved faster.

"Nooooo!"

Her single cry echoed across the cavernous room.

Chapter 7

Winnie spread a thin layer of Krema peanut butter on a thick slice of bread, added apple jelly to the second piece and handed the sandwich to the boy standing in front of her. "There you go, Johnny. And here's an apple to go with it."

"Thank you, Miss Tuttle." When he tore into the sandwich, Winnie wished she could give him two or three more sandwiches.

Did you say a blessing? The question tripped on the end of Winnie's tongue, but she didn't have the heart to scold him. When the pastor preached about the hungry at church, Winnie's thoughts turned to Johnny. First fill his stomach, and then he might think about God.

The next child, Johnny's sister Irene, slipped by with a shy thank you. Unlike her brother, she took her time with each bite, stretching the food as far as possible.

"Can I have some of your sandwich?" Johnny asked.

Winnie looked up as Johnny bumped his sister's elbow.

"No." Irene pinched off another tiny bite and popped it into her mouth.

Did they have anything to eat between their daily meals at the church? Winnie doubted it. Come winter, the pastor had mentioned offering hot soup and a spot on the floor to sleep. He would open the church doors now, but not everyone approved.

The door opened, revealing a slender woman with tired-looking blond hair and two small children in her arms. Her eyes flittered about, taking in the scene before her. She slipped furtively around the edge of the tables until she reached the serving window. "Can I get some food for my children?"

Winnie's heart hurt. People like this woman hated to ask for help until their children's needs drove them to it. Up close, the newcomer looked younger than at a distance, in spite of the weary lines already forming around the corners of her eyes. No man accompanied her; a lot of men had abandoned their families or gone elsewhere in search of work.

Winnie put together three sandwiches, added an apple, dished some applesauce into a bowl for the baby and poured a tall glass of milk. As she gave the mother the tray, she said, "Eat something yourself, too."

The serving line petered out shortly after that, and Winnie made a sandwich for herself and poured a glass of water. An empty spot opened up across the table from the mother with her children, and Winnie sat down.

Winnie engaged the baby in a game of peek-a-boo, and soon the little girl was laughing. The little boy, who couldn't be much older than two, smiled shyly, and Winnie played the game with both of them.

"What's your name?" Winnie asked.

The child stuck his thumb in his mouth and buried his head against his mother's shoulder.

"His name is Eugene." His mother wiped her mouth with a napkin and bit into the apple with a satisfying crunch.

"He's adorable. How old is the baby? She's a girl, yes?"

The mother nodded. "She'll be eight months old tomorrow." A small smile lit the woman's face. She must have been beautiful, once. "Won't you, my Olive?" She kissed the top of the baby's head.

"Olive, that's a nice name. Pat-a-cake, pat-a-cake, baker's man."

The baby's eyes lit up and she brought her hands together. When they finished the rhyme, Olive reached for Winnie. "May I?"

"Yes." The mother handed the baby to her.

Winnie wondered about the woman's story, but she had learned to let the person across the table set the pace of the conversation. "My name is Winnie Tuttle."

"I'm Danielle, Danielle Parnell."

"I'm glad to meet you, Danielle. You know you are welcome to come at any time."

Tears welled in Danielle's eyes. Her son's eyes kept straying to the half sandwich Winnie had left. "May I?" At Danielle's nod, Winnie gave him the plate.

"What do you say?" Danielle's tears dried as quickly as they had started.

"Thank you." The words came out muffled as he devoured the sandwich. Danielle wiped crumbs from his mouth.

"Winnie, can you help us in here?" Pastor Rucker asked.

"Maybe I'll see you later." Winnie returned to the kitchen. As she sudsed up the water and began the dishes, she prayed by name for each person who'd come through the serving line. Today she ran out of dishes before she had prayed for everyone, and she tacked on a "and God, take care of everyone else" at the end.

"Thank you, Winnie. And thank your sister for the extra milk." Pastor Rucker said the same thing every day.

"You're welcome." Winnie tapped her toe on the concrete, deciding to extend the invitation Preston had given. "Do you think the children here would enjoying ice skating? I've asked Preston, and he said he's willing to open up the ice for free, and he even has a bunch of old skates the kids could use."

Pastor Rucker smiled. "What a wonderful idea! You'll have to get the parents' permission, of course."

Winnie clapped her hands. "Great! I'll get it set up with Preston and the parents."

She skipped out of the church and down the road. Early that morning, she had endured yet another grueling skating session. As promised, Frank had proven to be a hard taskmaster, as stingy with praise as Scrooge was with pennies. Right now, she was heading home, where they still saw her as the baby sister, not old enough for adult responsibility in spite of her years.

Only at the soup kitchen, working with the man who had led her to the Lord years ago, did she feel as if she made a difference. She looked up at the sky. "I know, God. I should be thankful I have time to help others. Clarinda has her hands full." Her sister—and her four children—waited for her at the house. If Winnie wanted to help someone, she need never leave the farm—something Howard reminded her about on a regular basis.

Frank took off his blade protectors as he waited at the edge of the ice. When Preston and Winnie had planned the skating party in mid-August, he hadn't known what to expect—nothing like this. Children of every size, from those barely walking to rowdy youths ready to race, tumbled around the ice. So many inexperienced skaters crowding the ice rink threatened Winnie's safety, not to mention his own.

Winnie stopped at the gate. "Isn't this great? Come out and join the fun." With a grin and a wave, she skated away.

As he watched, she bent over a little girl of maybe three years, tottering on her skates. That might be her niece, Clarinda and Howard's youngest. Wallace approached the gate, holding the hands of a little boy who must be his son. In the five years since Frank had left, Wallace had married and fathered one child. Multiply that by changes across the community, and Frank didn't know half the people on the ice today.

Listening to Winnie's sparkling laughter, Frank realized anew what attracted him to her. She brought joy to everyone around her, giving without any thought of getting anything back. He could learn a lesson from her.

Wallace struggled off the ice with his son and sighed. "Phew. I didn't know skating at zero miles an hour could be so tiring." He brushed his hair back off his forehead. Winnie flew past again and waved. "You'd better get out there before Winnie drags you onto the ice."

Frank frowned. Wallace was acting as if that confrontation at the farmhouse last month had never happened. "You're not mad at me for coaching her?"

Wallace lifted his boy into his arms. "No, of course not. Although I confess, we need her help more than ever. Mary Anne wanted to come today, but she's not feeling very well."

"Yes, I heard congratulations are in order."

"Daddy, skate!" The boy tugged at Wallace's shirt.

"Not yet, squirt. Daddy has to rest." Wallace headed toward the benches while Frank stepped onto the ice.

Seconds later, a skater dashed past Frank, pushing him against the wall. The boy glanced over his shoulder. "Sorry, Mr. Sawtelle!" It was Howie, the oldest Finch boy.

Frank watched as Howie's brother, Arthur, followed.

Winnie stopped Howie to warn him. "There are *children* here."

"I'll be careful." The boy puffed out his chest, probably proud that Winnie had implied he wasn't a child himself.

Then again, when Frank was the boy's age, he was beating adults in figure skating competitions. The way he had thrown himself into skating at such a young age, he had gone from fun to serious training before reaching his teens. His childhood didn't resemble his contemporaries' very much.

Winnie balanced training with other responsibilities better. Today she sparkled at the center of the party. She joined Frank at the gate. "I apologize for my nephew. If he does that again, I'll make him leave the ice for a few minutes."

A boy and a girl of about ten made it to the gate. "Miss Tuttle!" Squealing, the girl flung her arms around Winnie and her skates went flying. Frank's heart stopped as they tumbled to the ice.

"Girls." Her brother looked disgusted.

"Don't worry, Johnny. Irene and I are fine." Standing, Winnie helped the girl to her feet before dusting herself off. She pointed to Frank. "This is Mr. Sawtelle, the famous skater I was telling you about."

Irene's blue eyes widened, while the boy shrugged his shoulders. "So, you skate good?"

Frank nodded. "People say so."

"Wanna race?" Johnny's eyes gleamed, the same look Frank had seen in every contender's face at Nationals, as well as every Hans Brinker hopeful who longed to win the local race.

"Johnny, Mr. Sawtelle is a figure skater," Winnie said. "Not a racer."

Johnny planted his hands on his hips and glared at

Frank. "He said he was good." To this boy, good clearly meant fast.

"I can skate faster than some." Now, why had Frank said that? He didn't want to race—did he?

He couldn't call the words back. When Johnny whistled, movement across the ice halted. "Mr. Sawtelle is going to race us!" Nash stuck his head out of his office window and looked down on the ice, shaking his head.

"You don't have to…" Winnie said.

Her question decided him. "I'll do it, on one condition. After the race, everyone who takes part gets a lemon drop for a prize. I brought a bag of candy with me."

"All right!" Johnny dashed off to tell the others, and Frank laughed as he saw word spread. Someone tugged at his shirt, and he looked down into Irene's face. "Can girls skate, too?"

"Of course," Frank said.

"Good." Irene fumbled in her brother's direction.

"You're holding a race?" Both of them turned to face Clarinda.

Arms akimbo, face bright pink, she was in full take-charge mode. "At least half of these children have never been on skates before. And did you see those skates…it's a wonder they're staying on their feet. Someone might be hurt." She turned to Frank. "I would expect you to have the good sense not to allow something like this."

"Actually, it was my idea." Frank looked at Howard, who had joined his wife. A good man and a good neighbor, he was very much a man of the earth. "Don't worry, Dr. Landrum is here." The physician had tended to Frank's various scrapes and illnesses as a boy, as well as any city doctor. If he had tended Frank's broken ankles, would things have turned out differently? "He's taken care of me more than once."

Howard started to speak, and Frank lifted his hand.

"Not that I expect anyone to get hurt." Around thirty youngsters had gathered around him, the littlest ones in their mothers' arms. A few timid girls waited around the sideboards, pointing and giggling. Others waited with the boys, daring anyone who crossed their paths.

Some of the boys wanted to beat him, and Frank smiled at the thought. Not that they could. But they might instead knock over the smaller children in their eagerness. He rubbed his chin. "Attention, everyone. Here are the rules for today's races."

The boy Johnny laughed. "We just have to skate down from one end of the ice t'other."

"There's too many of us to skate at one time. First the smallest ones will skate. Anyone who's no taller than the sideboard," Frank said.

Children lined up along the sideboard, and he divided them into two groups. The taller children, he chased off the ice. "Now wait your turn."

He spaced the remaining half-dozen children several feet apart so they could skate without running into one another. He nodded at Winnie. She said, "On your mark… get set…go."

Keeping pace, Frank skated down the ice, ready for any accidental spills. The only child he had met—the youngest Finch girl, Norma—looked so much like Winnie that he felt as though the calendar had turned back a few years. When she crossed the finish line in last place, she and Winnie shared matching smiles as she accepted a lemon drop and a hug.

The second group, mostly elementary school students, came next. Since there were fifteen children in the group, Frank divided them again, into boys and girls.

"Ah, c'mon, Mr. Sawtelle, I can skate as good as them boys," Irene said.

Frank smiled. "I expect you can, but there's too many

to have you all on the ice at one time. We don't want you bumping into each other."

Irene sprinted to the front of the girls. After she crossed the line first, she pranced in front of her brother. "Bet you can't beat me!"

Johnny stuck out his tongue at her before joining the line of boys. The determination on their faces, even the six-year-olds, tickled Frank. Johnny and Arthur led the pack while the spectators cheered.

The smallest skater bumped into the sideboard and fell down. Tears spilled down his cheeks and he repeated a word not often heard on Nash's ice.

Frank skated over to check for injuries. "Are you all right?"

He stood on unsteady feet. "I'm okay."

"That ice is rough until you get used to it." Frank checked the boy; he was shaken, but no harm was done.

"Can I have a lemon drop?" His lower lip trembled. "I didn't finish the race."

"Of course." Frank gestured for Winnie, but before she made it to his side, Johnny appeared. He held an unwrapped lemon drop in his hand. "Here. You take mine."

That's why Winnie worked at the soup kitchen. For moments like this.

Chapter 8

"So, what are your plans for tomorrow?" Danielle, the woman Winnie had first met almost a month ago at the beginning of August, quizzed Winnie as she dried a chipped glass. "Any more skating days?"

Winnie shook her head. "We'll have another party soon, though, maybe in October. You should come next time."

"It's not for me." Danielle put the glass in the overhead cabinet. "My babies are too little."

Winnie glanced over her shoulder. Olive crawled around the floor and Eugene played his unique rhythm on the soup pot, using a wooden spoon. "It won't be long before Eugene can give it a try."

Danielle grabbed the next glass and held it up to the light. "I know you're crazy about figure skating, but not all of us like the ice."

For someone who didn't like the ice much, Danielle knew a lot about figure skating, such as the difference between an axel and a toe loop. Whatever her story was,

Winnie knew as little about her as she did the day Danielle first arrived.

Winnie looked at the church kitchen, satisfied that it was spotless, as usual. The church elders couldn't complain about wear and tear on the building. She glanced at the clock and sighed. "I'd love to stay and talk, but…"

"You're wanted at home. It's okay. We'll be fine." Danielle washed the pot her son had used as a drum. "I'll see you on Monday, then, Lord willing."

Winnie didn't understand why a woman who knew the Lord stayed home from worship services, but it was none of her business. After kissing the two babies, she headed out the door.

As she crossed the square, Wallace came out of the mercantile. "Oh, good. I was afraid I'd missed you. Come on with me. Mary Anne's in a bad way. Clarinda knows, so it's okay."

Stifling annoyance at being told what to do, Winnie climbed in the car beside her brother and nephew. An empty candy wrapper brought a smile to her face; the chocolate was already melting in little Carl's mouth.

"You like candy, don't you?" She couldn't help but love the miniature version of her brother. That same puzzled expression had appeared on Wallace's face many times. His bright eyes and innocent smile brought joy to her heart. "There's nothing that's more hopeful than a new baby. As long as we have precious little ones like this, I feel like God is smiling down on us, no matter what doom and gloom I read in the newspapers."

When they crested the rise, they could see the mountains in the distance. Winnie hummed the tune to "Faith Is the Victory," the way her mother always had at that point in the road. It was one of the clearest memories she had of her parents. "I wonder what our parents would think of me skating."

Wallace puffed out his cheeks. "I know what Great-Grandma Clara would say. Finish your education first."

"I know. But what about Daddy? Or Mama?" Winnie loved Aunt Flo, who was the headmistress, but Winnie had chafed at the discipline of the boarding school. Continuing in that environment for four more years didn't appeal to her at all. She'd had her fill of dorm life and all-night study sessions before she even reached high school.

Wallace pushed his glasses back up on his nose. "I suspect they would have been as proud as a papa rooster. After Mom lost a couple of babies, they spoiled you rotten."

"Did not." Winnie's body tensed, and Carl looked up at her with those pretty eyes. "Sorry, Carl."

Wallace took the empty candy wrapper, balled it and threw it into a trash bag they kept handy in the car. "You got a lot more than candy when they took you to the store."

"Did not," she repeated, but this time she smiled.

"Mom taught you how to skate. She took you down there nearly every day, and you kept begging to go back. I don't know if you remember much about those years."

Oh, Winnie remembered, all right. Too young to keep up with Frank, she'd watched him with helpless adoration.

"In fact, you had a big crush on Frank, if I remember correctly." Wallace flashed a grin at her. "You're spending a lot of time with him these days. Is there anything I need to know about?"

She should have seen that question coming. With a guilty thought of the times they'd skated hand in hand, practicing steps together, she shook her head. "No. He's my coach, that's it. And he's tough, tougher than Preston ever was."

Wallace glanced at her. "So, he doesn't let you get away with anything. Like my editor. Good."

They turned onto the road that led to the cabin. "What kind of help do you need today?"

Wallace listed enough to keep her busy for the rest of the day and into tomorrow. She was in for another late night, making her wonder if she would get more sleep in a dorm. Her plans for visiting Louise vanished, again. Hopefully her friend would make it to church tomorrow, so they could at least give each other a hug.

Early Sunday morning, Frank knocked on the door to Louise's room.

"Come in," Louise called.

His sister sat on the edge of the bed, shivering in spite of wearing a nightgown heavy enough for Vermont's winters.

Although Frank found the early morning breeze refreshing, Louise probably preferred greater warmth. He shut the window. "So, you're not coming with us today?"

She shook her head. "Say hello to everyone for me, will you? Especially to Winnie?" Her voice caught, a rare indication of how much her isolation cost her.

"Do you want me to invite her over here for dinner? Mom would love to have guests."

"She's so busy…and I look like this." In spite of Louise's negative response, the longing in her eyes gave a different answer.

"I'll ask her. In my opinion, she could use a break from that family of hers." He walked to the door.

"Not to mention her skating coach," Louise called after him as he closed the door behind him.

Frank couldn't deny that. Winnie might not want to spend her free day with him, but he was counting on her desire to see Louise. She hadn't yet returned the visit from the Sunday when the Sawtelles went to the Finch farm. Why, when they were girls, they were inseparable. The footpath they created still existed between their farms.

Before long, he headed for church with Pa and Mom in their horse-drawn wagon. He didn't mind the walk, but it wore his mother out. Her dresses fit looser these days, and Pa's belt was cinched tighter, his suspenders holding his pants halfway up his chest. Frank had returned to find his family had shrunk, both physically and financially.

The church came into view, as well as various members of the Finch clan spilling out of their truck. When Winnie looked up, he waved. He enjoyed seeing her in her Sunday clothes; the rest of the week she wore practical jeans to work on the ice. The hat was probably considered fashionable, but he didn't care for it. It covered her unruly hair so that only the ends stuck out. He preferred her more windblown look.

He wanted to deliver the dinner invitation before other demands were made on her time. Perhaps he could convince her family to give her a break. He trotted over while Winnie watched her youngest niece climb over the edge of the door and drop down. "I did it, Aunt Winnie."

"Yes, you did."

Now he remembered. This niece wanted to imitate her aunt on the ice. The way Winnie interacted with her nieces and nephews, he knew she'd be a good mother someday. He could see her with a passel of kids circling her on the ice, practically born on skates, following in their parents' footsteps, with dark curly hair and a certain swagger.

He shook that thought out of his mind. No international-level hopeful, athlete or coach, could indulge in fantasy. No sensible person would start a family in times like this, not without any inkling of how to provide for one, when the family farm might slide out of their control any day.

Frank wrenched his thoughts back to the present. "Winnie, can you join us for dinner today?"

As soon as Frank saw the look pass between Winnie and her sister, Frank knew his invitation sounded like a date. "I mean…Louise said…" He couldn't get the words out.

"I'll catch up with you in a minute." Winnie waved

Clarinda away, allowing her a moment of privacy with Frank. "Is Louise okay?" She looked around the wagon. "She didn't come with you today, did she?"

Frank shook his head. "No, and I know she's missing you."

Winnie smacked her forehead with the back of her hand, one of those unpretentious gestures that endeared her to him. "I keep meaning to get over for a visit but…" Dropping her hand, she straightened her shoulders. "No excuses. She's my best friend. I should have made time to visit. Of course I'll join you after church."

"Are you sure Clarinda and Mary Anne won't mind?" *Please say no.*

"I'll put all the kids to bed tonight. Read Norma her favorite bedtime story twenty times over if I have to." Winnie laughed. "Don't worry, I'll be there for practice tomorrow morning in plenty of time."

During the service, the pastor continued his study of James, warning against becoming a master and misusing the tongue. "The word *master* translated means *teacher* today. Even today, advanced academic degrees are called 'masters.'"

Frank's mind skipped away. As Winnie's coach, he was the "master" in their relationship. Unlike the teachers James referred to, the pupil would be judged harshly if she failed at competition. It might matter to him if he wanted to pursue a career as a figure skating coach, but he didn't. His only concern was how well Winnie did at the competition.

He glanced in her direction. Her Bible lay open, with sermon notes jotted in the margins. *Lord, let her do well. Not for my sake. But for hers.*

The ceiling seemed to bind his prayer to the earth. He looked around the congregation. The same people attended church that did before he moved away. Did they struggle with issues of life, faith and victory, as he had in recent years? Surely he wasn't alone in his feelings of futility.

Then again, few people from his hometown had risen as high as he had—or fallen as far. It hurt. If he truly cared for Winnie, he would discourage her from pursuing such a slippery path.

Another glance at her reminded him that whether he helped her or not, she would pursue her dream. All he could do was to ease the way for her.

Chapter 9

"It's so beautiful out here." Louise lifted her too-pale face toward the sun. Toodles lay in her lap, her head resting on her mistress's arm. "Thank you for coaxing me outside."

Winnie had joined her friend on the bench in the flower garden. "A little fresh air and sunshine will do you good."

A cable-knit sweater more suitable for a cool spring day rested on Louise's thin shoulders, but she shivered as a light breeze brushed across her face. She tugged down her dress to cover more of her legs. "Times like this, I envy my grandmother. She wore a floor-length dress year round, always plenty warm."

Too warm for my tastes. "My great-grandma Clara would disagree with you. I remember her wearing bloomers. How silly she looked in those things." Winnie lifted the close-fitting hat from her head, baring her sweaty head to the breeze. "It's nice to sit for a little while. At home I'd be running after Norma or Carl and peeling potatoes. Even here, I feel like I should be inside, helping your mother."

"Relax. Enjoy yourself." Louise smiled. "Sitting here with you brings back memories. Do you remember how at school Miss Garrett tried to pound poetry into us?"

Winnie groaned. "'Love is not love which alters when it alteration finds.' I can still quote the whole sonnet. It's a beautiful thought, but she made me hate Shakespeare."

Louise laughed. "I have discovered a poet, or I should say, poetess, whom I thoroughly enjoy—Emily Dickinson. She wrote short, pithy things that are easy to understand. 'If I can stop one heart from breaking, I shall not live in vain.'" Louise closed her eyes. "You do a lot more of that than I can, with your work at the soup kitchen, helping people who have lost all hope."

"It's true about some of them, but with others, why, their faith is stronger than mine is. They say God only gives good gifts, even now. They call the soup kitchen a 'blessing.'" Tears came into her eyes. "Compared to them, I have so much. They're the ones who are blessing me." Winnie bent over and pulled a gladiolus toward her, breathing deeply. The garden was past full flower, as summer dwindled into fall. In two weeks' time, leaves would carpet the ground.

"Before we go inside," Louise said in a high-pitched, girlish tone. "Tell me what's happening with you and that bull-headed brother of mine."

The question jerked Winnie out of the relaxed state of mind she enjoyed in the garden. "He's coaching me. He doesn't seem to think much of my chances." She bit her lip. The truth was, she could use a bit of encouragement.

After scooting closer to Winnie, Louise leaned in as if she had a secret to tell. "That's not how I see it. He likes you, Winnie."

Winnie huffed. "No, he doesn't. Work, work, work, that's all we do."

Louise giggled. "You silly goose."

The conversation brought a sparkle to Louise's hazel eyes. A lover of romance, she had dragged Winnie to several romantic comedies—charmed by Maurice Chevalier in *The Love Parade,* pining with the luminous Mary Pickford in *Coquette*. How long ago that seemed.

"We should go to Burlington one of these weekends and see a movie. It's been too long." Surely Winnie could scrape together enough money to go.

"Oh, I don't think I could go. But you should go with Frank, instead." Louise smirked.

As if called by her words, Frank appeared at the door leading into the garden. "Did I hear my name?"

"Winnie was saying how much fun it would be for the two of you to go to a talking picture sometime soon."

Winnie scowled. That wasn't what she had said at all.

Louise ignored her protest. "You both need a break. Say you'll go. They say the new Charlie Chaplin movie, *City Lights,* is wonderful, even though it's not a talkie."

"I think I could manage that." Frank surprised Winnie with his answer.

When Frank smiled that way, how could she say no? "I'll have to ask what time is best for the family."

"Good. Mom says dinner is ready." Offering his arms to both women, he led them inside.

Frank didn't know what Louise and Winnie had talked about in the garden last Sunday, but the conversation had done his sister good. During the past week, her eyes had sparkled more often, and she giggled and chattered like the girl he remembered.

Winnie cheered up everyone she came in contact with. If he could only get her skating to mirror what he saw inside her. Combine her heart with her technique and she would be unstoppable. But first she needed to relax. The trip to the movies Louise had suggested was a great idea.

In spite of the family's financial struggles, Mom's face had brightened when he told her about the trip to the movies. Perhaps wedding bells rang in her imagination; she tended to hear them if he so much as glanced in a girl's direction.

"Mom, let me go." She was straightening the collar on his suit jacket. "Don't make more out of this than what it is. A break, to help her skate better. That's all."

"First dinner at her house, then a movie…there will be more." Mom tugged on his tie a final time and stood on tiptoe to kiss his cheek. "You look fine. Louise approves." Louise nodded from her seat on the couch.

Frank studied his reflection in the mirror over the fireplace. Not bad, he decided. He had kept his skating figure in spite of retiring from the sport. With a fresh shave and a splash of Aspen aftershave, he almost felt ready for a date. A non-date.

"She knows it's your birthday. She asked me about your favorite cake recipe." Mom studied him, a finger on her lips. "Do not embarrass me, eh?"

"Never, Mom." He kissed the top of her head. "But if I don't leave, I will be late, and that will never do."

"One last thing." Louise handed him a bouquet of gladioli. "Take these. She was smelling them in the garden last week."

Frank studied the bunch of pink flowers. "She will like these, I'm sure. Thank you."

"Gladioli means you are giving her your heart," Mom said.

Not responding to that final volley, Frank walked to the waiting Model T. Winnie's sister-in-law Mary Anne kept it running, more than any skill on their part. Mom had cleaned the inside earlier in the week. Frank had teased Louise into washing the outside. Just to see her outdoors had done him good, and she looked happier, as well.

Winnie had called this morning to say she had returned to Clarinda's house after spending a few weeks helping her sister-in-law through a difficult pregnancy. In spite of Winnie's many commitments, she never missed morning practice, not even when her nephew was running a fever and she had spent the night awake with him.

"Skating keeps me from going crazy," she had said. He believed it.

The Ford ate up the distance between their two farms and he arrived before his nerves got out of hand. When he pulled into the yard, Howie and Arthur were running around, hollering and holding their stomachs as if they hurt. Lord, let there be nothing wrong that will keep us from going to Burlington tonight. Winnie would drop their plans in an instant if she thought her family needed her.

When he opened the car door, his worries lessened. The boys were laughing, not screaming, almost howling with glee. When they saw him, they burst into a renewed fit of laughter.

Intrigued, Frank approached them. "Share the joke."

Arthur opened his mouth, but he could only laugh. A full minute passed before their laughter subsided to the point where he could gasp out an answer. "Can't tell you— have to—see."

Who could guess what ten-year-old boys found funny? From what he remembered, it could be bathroom humor or something about a girl. Maybe that was it, laughing at the thought of Aunt Winnie going on a date.

Eager to see Winnie, Frank strode to the door. As he approached, a strong odor emanated from the kitchen. *Smoke.*

The back door slammed and he raced around the house. Mary Anne stumbled out first, hand over nose and mouth. Wallace followed close behind with Carl in his arms. Clarinda chased her two girls out of doors.

Howard ran from the fields, chest heaving with the effort. "What's the smoke? Is something on fire?"

Where was Winnie? Wallace turned to face the door.

Before he reached the steps, a broom handle poked through the doorway, something blackened swinging from the end. Winnie followed, her face smeared black, coughing, taking the burnt offering straight to the horse trough.

Out of the corner of his eye, Frank saw the boys pointing and laughing, but Clarinda shushed them. Winnie's obvious distress shut all other sounds and sights out, and he drew near.

As he approached, he saw a glimmer of steel attached to a sole....

Ice skates.

Lunging forward, he plunged his arms into the water, hoping against hope that he was mistaken in what he expected to find.

Beside him, Winnie spoke in a strangled voice. "Don't. If you take it out before it cools down, the leather might break apart."

The swirling, blackened water indicated there was little chance of rescue, but Frank withdrew his hands. They stared into the water, sharing a silent agony.

When he couldn't stand the silence any longer, he said, "You needed a new pair of skates before Nationals in any case. I've been thinking about how to make it happen. We'll just have to do it sooner, that's all."

"It's useless." Winnie shook her head. "I know Norma likes to hide things in the oven. Clarinda always reminds me to check before I turn the oven on, but I was too busy making your birthday cake. Of all the stupid, irresponsible things to do." From the set of her mouth, Frank guessed that a few words Winnie would never use in public stampeded through her mind. "That's what I get for chasing after some foolish dream."

When she looked at Frank, he saw the care she had taken with her appearance, evident beneath the sooty cheeks. A pair of tiny red bows held her hair back from her forehead, and a touch of lipstick brightened her lips. "You won't mind if we don't go to see the movie, will you? We have the meal ready, mostly, if the smoke didn't ruin it." With that, she did an about-face and walked back into the kitchen.

Snickers continued to escape from the boys like steam from a teapot until Frank looked at them. "Your aunt is feeling pretty bad about now. Imagine if you lost something important to you."

"Aw, shucks, Mr. Sawtelle, we didn't mean any harm."

"I know that. And she did look funny, poking out the skates on the broom handle." Frank allowed himself a grin. "But keep your giggles away from your aunt. Can you do that?"

"Yes, sir!" Howie saluted before heading in the direction of the barn. Arthur ran after him.

"We might as well go back inside, by the front door." Clarinda walked to the corner, and Frank followed. The odor of burned leather hung lightly in the air, lessened by leaving both doors open. Now the traditional Saturday evening aromas of baked beans and good brown bread were evident, as well.

A little bit of smoke never did beans any harm. He grinned, and then a sober expression returned to his face.

Burned skates were a different matter.

Chapter 10

Winnie's body refused her order to sleep late on the Monday morning after burning her skates. Shortly after four, the same time as usual, she woke up. She stayed in bed as the minute hand passed five minutes...ten...a quarter after. Her eyes refused to stay shut.

She couldn't, she wouldn't go to the ice rink today. What was the point? She had no skates. She couldn't practice. If she missed rehearsal time, she could kiss her dreams goodbye. Regular practice didn't guarantee success, but laziness was the surest, shortest route to failure.

Forget breakfast. Today she had no desire to go to the kitchen, to surround herself with reminders of her colossal mistake. It was a good thing she had left a couple of cookies—Clarinda's comfort food, baked last night—to eat this morning.

After freshening up, she opened her Bible to the fortieth chapter of the book of Isaiah. "Comfort ye my people, saith your God." She remembered the tenor's voice rising in the recitative from Handel's *Messiah,* which she had listened to over and over again on the Victrola. Today the words mocked her. Who would God send to comfort her— someone who sold ice skates?

Something rattled her window ever so slightly, then repeated itself. When she looked up, she saw Frank's face peeking up over the sill. With a grin, he waved hello. Grabbing the robe on the chair next to the bed, she slipped it over her gown and climbed out of bed. Lifting the window high enough so they could talk, she whispered, "What are you doing here?"

"I figured you would think you could skip practice this morning." In spite of his scolding words, he was smiling. "I'm here to make sure you come. We're going to work so hard, you're going to wish you were on the ice."

"It's pointless." She pulled back from the window.

He shook his head. "Do you want me to raise my voice so everyone hears?"

His volume increased on the last three words, and she lunged forward. "Keep quiet. I'll be right out." She shut the window and pulled down the blinds.

To think of the days she and Louise had dreamed about boys throwing stones against their windows. She never expected to find Frank at her window, driving her crazy with his impossible talk, as if training and international competition were still a possibility. She ran her brush through her hair, not that it helped after the way she had tossed and turned last night. Her hair resembled a dried-out dandelion.

Grabbing a pair of fresh blue jeans from her drawer, she put on a blouse and added a cardigan in case of morning chill. She was still grumbling when she met Frank outside.

Taking in her disheveled appearance, he grinned. "Thought you'd get off easy this morning, huh? Come on, let's run."

She bared her teeth at him and started running down

a dirt path in the direction of the family cemetery. At least she had good shoes for running, gym shoes from her last year at the Seminary, about a year old. Frank's shoes showed a little more wear, as if he ran frequently. Breathing easily, he said, "On the days I can't get to an ice rink, I find that running helps. Keeps my breath even and my legs strong."

She sped up a bit, and soon they reached the family graveyard. She touched the gatepost as she passed it. Her ancestors' blood ran in her veins, whether they would approve of her or not.

"This way." Frank broke away from the path and headed east, in the direction of the Bumblebee River. Winnie fell into a rhythm, her feet moving heel-to-toe, raising one leg, pounding forward, repeating the same action with the other leg. Her arms pumped at her sides, and her breathing increased ever so slightly.

Frank didn't speak again, and Winnie heard water rippling ahead. The Bumblebee River had served as highway, barrier and crossroads for the Tuttle family for centuries, but she mostly enjoyed it as her favorite summer haunt. "You're headed for the old fishing hole."

He laughed. "Got me."

They never had gone fishing after they talked about it back on the Fourth of July. Winnie had hoped for Louise to get well enough to join them. When that didn't happen, practice and the rest of life had taken over. Frank reached the riverbank first.

"We don't have fishing poles." Winnie sank down on the same rock she had used on many a day.

"No, but it's a good place to grab a bite to eat. I took you from the house before you ate breakfast."

Her stomach growled at the reminder. A half-eaten cookie didn't count.

"I brought along some buttered bread and a canteen."

He took a large napkin from his knapsack, unfolded it and handed her a thick slab of bread with butter on it. "When you're done with that, I've got another one with apple butter."

"Thanks." They ate in companionable silence, studying the sunrise sparkling on the water. "If we could put the gold in that water in the bank, we'd be rich as Croesus."

"Then we might not be able to enjoy a simple breakfast of bread and butter, and good company by the river."

"I'd like a chance to try it. Being rich, I mean. Money may not buy happiness, but it can buy survival. Even ice skates." She sighed. "You haven't mentioned the skates. What's the point of training? I can't afford another pair of skates. Even before yesterday happened, I had thought about new skates, but I couldn't figure out a way." She shook her head. "It's impossible."

"God doesn't know the meaning of impossible," Frank said.

The depth of despair on Winnie's face hurt Frank, but he hoped he could show her something new he had learned. "Our town brags about its history, about the victories in battle at Fort Ticonderoga and chasing after those thieves after St. Albans Raid. We sing 'Faith Is the Victory' as if the faith of our forefathers determined the outcome of those wars. The thing is, we face an even bigger battle now. For whatever reason, your part, maybe even our part, is to get you to Nationals. Maybe even beyond. Faith will be our victory, as much as it was theirs."

Winnie sniffled. "Faith doesn't buy skates."

"No." Reluctantly Frank stood. If he didn't move soon, Winnie might bolt before he could put his plan into action. "But until God gets you another pair of skates, we'll continue training as if we know it's going to happen." He held out a hand and helped her to her feet. "I'll meet you tomorrow morning for a run, and then we'll go to the rink. I have some ideas of things we can do while we wait." He cocked his head to the south, in the direction of the bridge. "Do you mind if I come into town with you today?"

The smile on her face rewarded him. "I'm not exactly dressed for the soup kitchen, but…why not? It might help someone realize they don't have dress up to receive help. Some people worry about that, you know. Pastor Rucker says a pretty face—" she blushed as she said it "—encourages them that there are still good things and good days ahead."

"Amen to that." They walked in the direction of the bridge. What would the soup kitchen be like? From what Winnie had said, a lot of people needed their services, from Maple Notch and around Chittenden County. He expected to run into people he had last met under happier circumstances, for both of them.

Maybe he would find more in common with the down-and-outers than he had ever considered. *Lord, open my mind and my heart. Let me see them as You do.*

Through the trees ahead he saw the underpinnings of the bridge, and beyond that, a shadow that indicated the cave famous for sheltering patriots during the Revolutionary War. "We need to climb the bank or else we'll come out underneath the bridge."

He climbed up first and helped Winnie over rocks and tree branches along the way up. A wind storm last night had ripped a few leaves from the trees, laying the first strips of color in the fall carpet.

Winnie's cheeks were pink, and her curly hair had twisted in its usual frenzy. The run had done her good. In spite of all his talk about trusting God to provide new skates, all night long he had worried over possible answers. Wait. Trust Me. That didn't mean he couldn't ask, did it?

"I can't get used to this new bridge. It's so much big-

ger, and concrete and steel can't take the place of wood."
Frank followed Winnie onto the span, their feet echoing
against the concrete floor.

Midway across she stopped where a one-by-six plank
was mounted on the wall. "This is the new courting board,
but it's just not the same. Wallace and Mary Anne carved
their initials here. And there's Bob and Kay Richardson.
You know them." She continued identifying all the initials
carved on the surface; it continued as the public newspaper
announcing courtships in the town. "But not everyone has
taken the trouble to add their initials and besides…" She
gestured to the two-laned width and high ceiling. "It's just
not the same as the old bridge. We lost more than a way to
cross the river during the flood."

Frank had missed that bit of excitement, when the
Bumblebee had flooded in November 1927, taking the
old bridge with it. "Progress. It giveth and it taketh."

About fifteen minutes later, they reached the town
square. "It won't be time to start serving for an hour or
so. I'm going in to help fix the meal."

"I want to help." He had warned his parents about the
change of schedule. Mom probably heard wedding bells.
"With your permission, I'll talk with the pastor about your
need."

"We can't ask…"

"We can ask him to pray. The whole town prayed for
me when I won Nationals. They'll want to do the same
for you, I'm sure."

"I suppose."

"I'll be down soon." He patted her shoulder in helpless
comfort before heading up the steps from the basement.
Light streamed through the stained-glass window of Jesus
on the Mount of Transfiguration. *He is my beloved Son, in
whom I am well pleased; hear ye him.* The Lord who could
make coins appear in the mouth of a fish could easily set

down a pair of skates in Winnie's closet, a Cinderella-fit for Winnie's feet.

The Lord who could make a coin appear also multiplied loaves of bread, but still there were thousands of people going hungry all across the country.

Staring at the window, he prayed out loud. "Lord, You know I'm not asking this for me, but for Winnie. She does so much for You. Her every thought, all day long, is how to help people around her. And You made her the way she is, with skating talent and the drive to compete." He looked up at the figure in the glass, wishing God would speak from a cloud as He did on the mountain.

Footsteps padded down the aisle, and Pastor Rucker joined Frank. "Sounds like you've got something on your mind, son."

Frank drew a deep breath. "How much do you know about Winnie's ice skating? What she hopes to do?"

"I know she went to the national championship last year. Reminded folks of you, of course. Is she going back this year?"

"She wants to." Frank laid Winnie's dreams bare, along with a great deal of his own soul. "And now she's accidentally burned her skates. No one has money to replace them, not in these times." He held his breath, fearing another Howard-like condemnation of such a wasteful use of time and money.

"How much does a pair of good skates cost?" The pastor smiled. "We might as well tell God exactly what she needs."

Chapter 11

Saturday morning Winnie stared hopelessly across the ice. The worn-out, left-over skates she had tried didn't hold up to the wear and tear of hour after hour on the ice. She and Frank had come every morning all week. Although she had hidden it from Frank, she cried on the way to and from the mill every day. His approach was sensible, if she ever expected to get back on the ice. But she was no closer to buying another pair of skates than she was when she burned them to a crisp last week.

"I've got the coffee ready," Preston called from his office.

Winnie waved. "Be right up." Bless Preston's heart. He had arisen this early—force of habit he said, but she knew better—every day when they hadn't even needed the ice. As long as they needed a place to train, he said, the mill was theirs.

Frank hadn't arrived yet, which surprised her a little. After trotting up the steps, she accepted a cup of coffee from Preston. "I don't see any purpose in keeping up this charade next week. My family always thought this was a foolish idea, and now they think I'm really crazy."

"Frank knows what he's doing." Preston drained his mug and added more coffee. "Made me dig out my old gramophone, didn't he?"

That part of Frank's revised morning routine made her smile. They danced together to the music. The scratchy sound caused by the dull needle didn't do the old recordings any good, but Frank kept bringing new ones. She didn't know where he had learned to dance so well—probably one of many skills acquired during his years away.

Some of the music they danced to—not to mention the dances themselves—might raise a few eyebrows in Maple Notch, but Preston didn't mind. No one would reveal their secrets, which hid nothing more dangerous than rhythm, melody, harmony and fun—not to mention hard work.

"Tiptoe through the tulips." She sang a line, and Preston made a circling motion with his hand, encouraging her to dance.

She obliged, first taking off her gym shoes. This song, done on tiptoe as if she were a ballerina, matched the lyrics. "Shades of night are creeping…" She lunged sideways, dragging her toes along the floor.

Frank slid through the door, set down a stack of recordings and joined the dance. "…scheming to get you out here."

At the last word, he swept her out the door, saluting Preston as they passed. They continued dancing, floating across the wooden boards.

Frank slid seamlessly into "I'm Looking Over a Four Leaf Clover." He used this one song to encourage her to practice spins and crouches and changing position, pretending she was looking for that elusive symbol of good luck. When they finished the second song, he said, "And yes, we have no bananas, but I have something else in mind today." He led her by the hand into the office.

Preston had spread the records Frank had brought across his desk, maybe a dozen in all. He grinned at Winnie as if they were holding a surprise birthday party and she was the guest. "It's time for you to choose."

She looked at the recordings, from artists as varied as Al Jolson, Louis Armstrong and Jimmie Rodgers. "What am I choosing?"

Preston looked at Frank. "You tell her."

"It's time for you to choose the music for your free skate." Frank ran his thumb over a fingernail.

She stepped back from the table. "My routine? I'm not even skating."

"Not yet." Preston tapped the edge of his mug with his fingers. "But you will be, and you might as well get ready." Steely blue eyes peered into hers, warning her to agree or else.

"So…pick your poison." Frank settled against Preston's desk.

Might as well play along. The songs ranged from happy to sad, thoughtful to fun. She kept returning to Jimmie Rodgers's "Waiting for a Train." The words always made her cry. "My pocketbook is empty and my heart is full of pain." Even though the song was popular before the market crash and the music was upbeat, it gained meaning as more and more hobos took to the trains, looking for the next place to call home. Her hand hovered over the record, then pulled away. She wanted music that would lift people up, not make them cry.

Her eyes lit on Leo Wood's "Climb a Tree with Me" and she giggled. "This one would be fun. It reminds me of the old fishing hole."

"Oh, come and climb a tree with me, as we climbed long

years ago." Frank took the record from the jacket and put it on the gramophone. "Lively. Good choice."

Time sped by as they discussed how to incorporate the required elements of the routine, which included jumps and spins and footwork to perform. As they listened to the recording, she could see the routine in her mind. She could almost feel the ice beneath her feet.

After the recording ended for yet another time, Winnie forced herself to check the clock. "It's time for me to leave."

Frank glanced up. "Is it that time already?" He shook his head. "Give me a minute, and I'll come down with you."

Winnie cleaned up the coffeepot while Frank took care of the gramophone, making a lot of noise in the process. Preston had disappeared downstairs a while ago. After Frank helped her into her cardigan, they clattered down the steps. "We sound like a herd of elephants today."

"How do you know? Have you ever been near a herd of elephants?" Frank opened the door at the bottom of the stairs.

"Surprise!" Irene darted forwarded, her arms full with a basket holding Indian corn and all the fall leaves they could gather this early in the season.

Winnie looked beyond them and saw dozens of youngsters waiting in the rink. "We need another skating lesson, and Mr. Sawtelle told us to come today," Johnny added. Most of the children had skates slung over their shoulders, the way they had seen her carry hers. She looked to Frank for an explanation.

Frank saw the confusion, the hurt on Winnie's face. Why hadn't he thought about that when he and the pastor concocted their plan?

"Good morning." Pastor Rucker's cheery voice called

from the door. "I've got lunches with me, for after the skating session."

Winnie looked down at her feet, then at the children, as if uncertain how to remind them of the reason she couldn't skate. "Perhaps Mr. Sawtelle can skate with you today...."

Irene poked Johnny in the side. "Tell her."

Johnny stood straight, all four-and-a-half feet of him, and planted his over-big feet on the floor. "Pastor Rucker told us you needed fifteen more dollars for a new pair of skates. We all gave a whole fifty cents each. If we didn't have the money, he found us jobs to do, to earn the money. Me, I swept out the store every day this week."

The pastor came forward, holding a bag. "Frank says these are good-quality skates."

Winnie's eyes grew wide, and so did her mouth, but no sound came out as she took the bag. She felt the heft of it in her hands, drew out the box and gasped when she read the brand name on the top. She pulled off the cover and pushed aside the tissue paper stuffed around the skates inside. Tears flooded her ears and streamed down her cheeks. "You shouldn't have. All that money..."

"You're always telling us to trust God, and He will provide our needs. I guess He must have thought you needed a pair of skates, Miss Tuttle." Johnny's chest puffed out, as if he had earned every penny himself—and he deserved to feel proud after the way he'd worked so hard.

"Put 'em on, Miss Tuttle." Irene edged closer. "I can't wait to see how they look."

Winnie stared at her feet, her finger running around the edge of the socks that Frank knew had a hole in one toe. Frank took the box from her hands and set it on the bench, then took her by the hands and led her to the bench.

Beneath the murmur of conversation and giggles, she whispered, "I can't accept these. The money they earned...

they need it for important things like clothes and a roof over their heads and food for their stomachs. I can't…"

Frank struggled to find a way to help her understand. "They are also human beings who need to help someone else. You. The Bible says it's more blessed to give than to receive, and it's their turn to give." Putting his words into action, he knelt in front of her and tugged the gym shoe off her foot. Wrapping her sock so her toe was covered, he pulled the boot of the skate over her foot. It slipped on easily, as if it had been custom-made, and he released a breath as he laced it up.

Winnie studied her feet as she turned them from side to side. "I feel like Cinderella."

"And it's time to go to the ball." Frank laced the other skate before helping her to her feet. "Time to test the glass slippers," he whispered in her ear as he pushed her onto the ice.

The children circled the sideboards, watching Winnie float across the ice. Tentative at first, she increased speed and turned into a backward skate, the wind blowing her curls across her face. Reaching center ice, she jumped into the air and rotated once, twice before landing one foot on the ice. The boys gave a cat whistle and the girls cheered.

"Who wants to go skating?" Frank called.

Thirty pairs of feet scrambled on the ice, and the party started.

Since the children had astounded her with the new skates almost a month ago, Winnie hadn't missed a minute of training time, inspired to greater efforts than ever. She scampered over the last few feet of the path to the old mill. "So let's climb a tree, you and me." The fishing hole wasn't far away. She was still whistling when she entered the mill.

"That you, Winnie? Come on up." Preston called from overhead.

Winnie waved and climbed the stairs, carrying the skates with her. Those skates had been receiving five-star treatment, with oil rubbed into the leather every night and the blades sharpened once a week. God had provided for her after she destroyed the last pair, and she vowed to take good care of their replacements. She wouldn't ask for another set for the rest of her life if she could help it.

Preston handed her a mug and a slice of cinnamon toast as she took a seat. "Frank's late," she said.

Preston stirred a bit of sugar into his cup. "No, he called. He can't make it today. Gave me a list of things to go over with you." He coughed, a harrumph coming from his throat. "As if I don't have eyes of my own to figure out what needs work."

Frank wasn't coming? Winnie set the cup back in her lap, her enthusiasm for the early morning session draining away. "He's not sick, is he?"

"Nope." Preston didn't elaborate, and Winnie didn't want to press.

She forced herself to eat and drink, although her taste buds didn't enjoy the food as much as usual. Preston handed her a sheet of lined yellow paper with his stark printing on it. "Work on footwork," it read. She sighed. Footwork, again. She could do the steps perfectly as long as Frank skated by her side, but as soon as he left, she missed the mark by an inch on either side more often than not.

Half an hour later, Winnie was attempting to complete a perfect figure eight.

"You can do it, just put your mind to it." Preston's advice had changed little over the past three years.

Winnie bit on her tongue to keep from making an angry retort. Frank's absence and her bad humor weren't Preston's fault. "I know." She worked her way down the ice, skating in double loops until she thought she would drop from dizziness.

The door burst open, bright sunlight streaming across the ice. Howard's voice called through the golden haze. "Winnie, come quick! Clarinda's in labor."

Chapter 12

The sun spread its rays across Winnie's face. She turned over once, then sat up straight. A glance at the clock confirmed her worst fears. Seven o'clock. She was late for practice, late for breakfast, late for...

Slowly she came back to her senses. Clarinda had given birth to twin girls the night before last. This was Sunday morning. She hadn't missed skating, not today, but she needed to start breakfast for the family.

After slipping into her bathrobe and a pair of slippers, Winnie scooted out of her room and headed for the nursery. The baby girls, born two months early, were as tiny as baby kittens, and far more helpless.

She pushed the door open with only the tiniest whisper of sound, so as not to disturb the babies. A flannel-clad leg came into view, and she heard the gentle creaking of a rocking chair. Howard.

"Clarinda?" His voice cracked.

"No, it's Winnie." She pushed the door open. Anita,

the dark-haired baby, lay in the bassinet. Evelyn nestled in her father's arms, almost nose to nose with him as he cradled her.

Winnie bent over the crib, brushing a thin strand of hair away from her niece's face. Anita chirruped and wiggled, settling back into a deep sleep. "She's so peaceful." Winnie pulled her bathrobe beneath her as she perched on the edge of the bed that shared the room with the bassinet.

Howard rocked without speaking, holding the smaller of the two girls. Evelyn didn't cry, and Winnie wondered why Howard continued to hold her. He was a loving father, of course, but he didn't spend much time cuddling his children. Since she wasn't fussing, Winnie expected him to go back to bed.

He stared in Winnie's direction without seeming to see her. When he blinked, tears appeared in his eyes.

"I heard crying, so I came in to check on them. If they're hungry, I bring them to Clarinda. Otherwise, I try to get them back to sleep. I changed Anita's diaper, and she fell asleep as soon as I laid her down. But Evelyn…"

A single tear rolled down his right cheek. "She felt cold, so I reached for her blanket, but then I saw that her little chest wasn't moving." Tears cascaded down his cheeks. "She's gone, Winnie. Our little angel is gone."

Winnie collapsed against the bed, and then struggled back to a sitting position. "Oh, Howard. Does Clarinda know yet?"

His body shook with quiet sobs. "No. This pregnancy was so hard on her…she can't go through this again."

That was their private business, but Winnie knew her sister would take the loss hard.

The children would awaken soon, racing down the stairs, ready to see their new sisters. Winnie had to act. "You go talk to Clarinda. I'll take care of the children for the morning. I'll stay home from church, in case you need me."

Howard staggered to his feet and headed to the door. "Leave it open a crack, so we can hear Anita if she cries. Oh, God, don't repeat this tragedy."

Winnie wished she had time to pray long hours, for her sister as well as her brother-in-law and the living baby. The remaining twin was so frail, she feared for her life. Clarinda had had a difficult labor, and recovery was taking longer than usual. This was a day when Winnie's prayers needed feet, as Aunt Flo liked to say. Winnie must put a smile on her face and take care of the children. She took advantage of the empty kitchen to put in a quick call to the parsonage to explain the situation.

"Tell Howard and Clarinda that we're praying with them," Pastor Rucker said. The phone call ended just as Howie rushed into the room.

From that point on, the morning ran in circles. Winnie stayed busy while not getting anything done. Over and over again she explained that, no, the children couldn't go see the babies. They were very sick. They couldn't see Mommy or Daddy this morning, either, not yet, not until they came downstairs.

After Winnie settled Norma down for her afternoon nap, a scowling Howie came up to her, arms crossed. "Something is wrong, Aunt Winnie. You can tell me."

Oh, how she loved this boy, trying so hard to be a man, but it wasn't her job to tell him the news. "You're right. But you have to wait for your father. Can I trust you to keep the little ones busy while your parents take care of other things?"

Howie slowly nodded. "I'll try, but Betty can be loud."

Winnie almost laughed. The boys made more noise, but they played outside most of the time. "Just remind her to be quiet."

Winnie kept the children in the parlor, and the boys played a game of Parcheesi. Norma rocked her doll, dressed in a long baby gown, and sang "Rockabye, Baby."

"You're so sweet, Evelyn," Norma said to her doll. "Your sister Anita has black hair like me and Aunt Winnie, but you have blond hair like Betty's." She kissed the top of the doll's head, wrapped her in a blanket and laid her on the floor. "I'm bored. I want to play with our real babies, upstairs."

As if in answer, the sound of heavy footsteps came from the stairway. Betty jumped up. "Daddy!" Winnie twisted in her chair and saw Howard crossing the floor.

Howard's tired face lifted in a smile, and he swung Norma up in his arms. Betty hugged his waist.

"I want to go see the babies. Can I?" Norma asked.

His shoulders sagged as he carried her into the parlor. "Not now, precious." He sat in his easy chair, settling Norma on his lap. "I have something to tell all of you."

Howie glanced at Winnie and she nodded. He crossed his legs and straightened his back. Betty leaned against her father's shoulder, and Arthur waited with a Parcheesi piece in his hand.

"You know our new babies have been sick."

Norma took her thumb out of her mouth. "Aunt Winnie wouldn't let me go upstairs and play with them."

Howard patted her back wordlessly.

"Is something wrong, Dad?" Howie put his fear into words.

Howard looked at his oldest son, his mouth searching for the right words. "Evelyn…has gone home to be with Jesus."

"But Jesus is in heaven," Betty said.

"He means she's dead." Howie put it into blunt words, his eyes open wells of sudden adult understanding. "Are Anita and Mom all right?"

"They're both asleep. I think they're going to be okay." He put Norma on the floor, but she clung to him. "Honey, I need to call…"

Winnie stood. "I'll take care of it. I already called the pastor. Do you want Dr. Landrum? Smithsons?" She cringed as she referred to the funeral home.

Howard nodded. "Thanks."

After that, the day passed in a blur. Pastor Rucker arrived at the same time as the funeral director, and Mrs. Rucker took over with the children. Winnie accompanied the doctor when he examined his two remaining patients.

Clarinda looked more peaceful than Winnie had expected. "I begged God to spare my girls, like David did. But now Evelyn has gone to a better place, and I have five living children to worry about." She kissed the top of Anita's head. "How is she doing, Dr. Landrum?"

"Let's see." The doctor listened to the baby's heart and lungs again before straightening. "She seems reasonably healthy, aside from being small. Keep her warm, feed her often, put her to sleep on her back. I will come back in three days to check on you, and of course, you can call before then if something goes wrong. And you, get as much rest as you can." Turning to Winnie, Dr. Landrum said, "She can count on you, can't she? You can take time off from the soup kitchen and your training?"

"Of course." A dozen gold medals couldn't make up for Evelyn's death or for the pain the family was suffering. She squeezed Clarinda's hand. "I'll be here as long as you need me."

On Monday morning, Frank went to the rink early. Although he hadn't seen Winnie at church yesterday, he hoped she could return to practice today. But Clarinda might still need her help at home.

The ice was empty when he entered, so he headed for

the second floor. When he reached the door to the office, he heard Nash speaking with someone.

Nash nodded at Frank as he came in, his shoulder holding the telephone receiver against his ear. "I'll explain to Frank, but it'd be best if you can go over to his house and tell him yourself." He listened for a few more seconds. "I understand. Come back as soon as you can." He hung up and turned to Frank. "Sad news, I'm afraid. One of Clarinda's twins died on Saturday night. Winnie will be home for a few days, taking care of things."

"One of the babies died?" Frank settled in a chair, shaking his head. "How terrible." The joy babies brought to the world was only surpassed by the sadness that accompanied their loss. "Is the other girl healthy?"

"She's tiny, but Dr. Landrum says she's healthy." Nash plunked his coffee mug on his desk, poured out a cup for Frank and leaned forward, his hands on his knees. "You look like someone who has a load on his mind."

Frank brushed his hands through his hair. Which was worse? The loss of a life when it had hardly begun, or the threat facing somebody fully known—and loved? Neither. Both. "It's Louise. She caught another cold two weeks ago, and she's in bad shape."

Nash nodded. He knew of Louise's fragility as a child as well as the recent setbacks that had brought Frank home and the possible loss of the farm. "Sorry to hear that. Anything I can do, 'sides pray?"

"My folks are talking about moving away from here. Selling the farm or leaving it for the bank if nobody wants it. Taking Louise to a place with more hospitals and special doctors. Dr. Landrum is good." Frank thought of his desire for his childhood doctor when his ankles shattered. "But he's reached his limit. He's suggesting Louise see a doctor in Boston. And he even has a lead for a job for Dad." He looked at Nash at last. "And me, if I want it."

Nash stood without speaking, walked to the window, where he looked over the ice. He didn't speak, but Frank had learned to respect his silences over the years. At last he spoke. "I won't tell you what to do. 'Sides that, you're a man now. Able to do your own thinkin'. Either decision is both right and wrong. I might tell you to follow your heart, but I suspect your heart leads you both ways." He turned around. "You always say you do your best thinking on the ice. Go out there now. I'll stay up here, praying with you."

Accepting his friend's wisdom, Frank slipped down the stairs, changed into his skates and glided onto the ice.

Skating the length of the rink, he mentally listed all the reasons he should go with his family. His duty. His responsibility. His role, as a man and a provider, to take a job and make the money that might pay for the help his sister so desperately needed.

Returning in the other direction, he asked himself why he should stay. Winnie didn't suffer from confusion over a choice between family and skating. As soon as the family need appeared, she jumped in to help. That should make the decision easier.

He turned backward and skated near the sideboards, making the circuit of the ice. But…she was counting on him.

More than that, he wanted her dreams as much as she did, maybe more. For her, for himself. In some strange way, he hoped to redeem his lost dreams through her.

More than that, if he was honest, he wanted Winnie.

What kind of husband material would he be if he abandoned his family when they needed him most?

Chapter 13

What a difference a week had made, Winnie mused as she walked to the kitchen to use the phone. Life and death, love and loss—the children had bounced back quickly. Howie seemed the most distressed at the loss of baby Evelyn, visiting the new grave a couple of times. Betty stayed content, helping Clarinda with the surviving twin. Wrapped in warm red flannel, Anita looked like the baby Jesus might have looked in his bundling clothes. Each time her strong cries woke Winnie during the night, she said a prayer of thanks for a living, breathing baby, able to demand that her needs be met.

As busy as the week had been, Winnie had missed her daily routine. Even more than the hugs of the children from the soup kitchen, she had missed the hours with Frank. She hadn't heard from any of the Sawtelles all week, which surprised her.

When Winnie reached the kitchen, she found Clarinda

on the phone. Cupping her hand over the receiver, her sister asked, "Do you need the phone?"

"I need to tell Preston to expect me in the morning."

Clarinda's mouth pursed in the small pout that accompanied any mention of Winnie's skating, but she nodded.

Winnie took her place at the kitchen table and picked up the Sunday paper, checking to see if the crossword puzzle had been completed yet. Of course it was, but someone had thoughtfully erased the words so someone else could try her hand at it. The first clue, for a three-letter word for "temple student," would take some thinking. She would look at the first "down" clue to see if she could get the first letter. A four-letter word for "where cookies might crumble." *Mouth,* except that had too many letters. Hmm, four letters. Oh, *oven.* That wasn't bad. That made the first letter for "temple student" an *O.*

While she was contemplating a four-letter word for "unaccompanied," Clarinda hung up the phone.

"Do you need to call anyone else?" Winnie held her breath, hoping she would say no. Talking with Preston was almost as good as showing up at the rink in the morning.

The phone rang several times before Preston picked up. "Ayuh."

Preston was short, as usual. No one had drilled telephone manners into him, unlike the graduates of the Maple Notch Female Seminary. *Finch residence, Winnie Tuttle speaking.*

"Preston, it's Winnie. I plan on coming back to the mill in the morning. I wanted to let you know, in case Frank doesn't call."

"Huh." Coming from Preston, the single word could signify anything from assent to an objection.

"That is, of course, unless you can't accommodate us." What if he couldn't? She reminded herself of what a blessing the year-round rink was. Few towns in the United

States had such a facility, let alone small communities such as Maple Notch.

"No, I don't have a problem. But have you talked with Frank since last Sunday?"

"No." The breath left Winnie's chest. Had something happened?

"You go on over to the Sawtelle farm. There's things goin' on, and it's not my place to tell."

Winnie hung up the phone but stayed seated at the table, her head buried in her hands. She wanted to call Frank right now and demand to know what had happened and if she could help. But the family had disconnected the phone as a nonessential service some time ago. Barring that, she wanted to rush over there tonight, but it was too late. Like good farmers, the Sawtelles practiced the truth of Ben Franklin's maxim, "Early to bed and early to rise makes a man healthy, wealthy and wise."

In the morning, then, before Frank got caught in the work of the day. Provided Frank was even there.

No, Preston would have told her if Frank had left town. Wouldn't he? She stared at the calendar on the wall, at the black cat perched atop a fence staring at a harvest moon, and wished she could make all her problems disappear by wishing on a star.

A future without Frank Sawtelle would be bleak indeed, even if she had never worn a pair of ice skates in her life.

Frank should have known this day would arrive when he came home in July. What little money he added to the household budget, he more than took away by eating food and using electricity and gas. And as the weather had grown colder, Louise's health had declined by the day.

They should have left long ago.

He leaned against the window, looking out on a scene that could grace a Currier & Ives sketch. A full moon rested on top of the trees as the sun struggled to push an arm of sunshine over the rim of the day. He had watched it from the same spot from day to day, season to season, year to year.

Sighing, he pulled down the blind against the distraction the scene afforded him, only to see other reminders of his past. His high school diploma hung next to his awards from his participation in Grange, when his father still held hope his oldest son would follow in his footsteps as a farmer.

His skating awards filled two shelves. The first one was from a dozen years ago, when he was all of twelve years old, skating against adults—and beating them. They had called him a phenom. That was Winnie's first competition as well, he had learned. And he had called her "little squirt." His mouth twitched with a smile.

That was a happy memory. He had made the jump to the adult ranks too soon, however, and he stumbled more than once, at state, then at all–New England, before he finally made it to Nationals in his senior year of high school. Still, his awards grew bigger by the year, as if the size symbolized their significance.

The final award, a plaque stating "National Champion, 1927," held pride of place on the fireplace mantel downstairs. He'd expected the gold medal he had earned at the tender age of nineteen to be the first of many. In 1928, he'd hoped to compete for gold in St. Moritz, Switzerland. Instead, a trio of Europeans swept the medal ceremony— Grafstrom of Sweden, Bockl of Austria and Van Zeebroeck of Belgium. Only Beatrix Loughran had brought home a medal, bronze, for the United States in figure skating.

While they competed, he lay in a hospital bed, recuperating from his broken ankles, praying that by some miracle he would be able to compete in the 1932 games. Now even his renewed dream of returning, as a coach if not a skater, had landed in the dust, along with the plaque downstairs.

He grabbed the medal from its hook on the wall and flung it on top of a pile of outgrown clothes and books he no longer cared for.

"Frank." Mom's voice floated up the stairs. "Winnie is here to see you."

Winnie? Glad he had dressed early, Frank trotted downstairs and met her in the parlor.

She looked so fresh, no indication of the hardships of the past week evident on her face. But worry was there, as well.

"Preston told me to come see you." She sat down on the nearest chair as if readying herself for a long discussion.

"Sit down with your guest." Mom bustled out of the parlor, and soon the sound of rattling china reached his ears.

"How are Clarinda and the baby?"

A radiant smile broke out on Winnie's face. "Oh, Frank. Anita is adorable. She is so tiny." The smile diminished. "She's wearing clothes Clarinda made for Norma's baby doll. Mostly she's just wrapped up in blankets, her tiny red face peeking out, her mouth moving, prying one eye open at a time. She's got a lot of hair, and it's dark." She touched her own hair as if for reference.

An image of a baby a lot like Anita, a pink bow holding a black curl away from her face, jumped into Frank's mind. He was peering over Winnie's shoulder, into the face of his daughter. *So let's climb a tree, you and me, and dream of baby land.* Pull back, his heart reminded him.

"She's already wormed her way into our hearts. I hate to think of anything happening to her." Winnie sank back against the cushion.

"We were all sorry to hear about the twin." Babies died, but each one was a tragedy. "Clarinda is recovering well, though, I take it?"

Winnie nodded. "Back on her feet, running around the house as if nothing had happened. She says keeping busy helps take her mind off the loss. She trotted out the old story about how one of our ancestors gave birth in a cave during the Revolutionary War, so she wouldn't complain."

Mom brought in two cups of coffee, with biscuits. "Thank you." Winnie bit into the first biscuit. "Delicious, as always." She dabbed the crumbs away from her mouth with her napkin.

They ate the biscuits, talking more about how the Finch children had taken the arrival of another sister—putting the girls in the majority in the household—while they consumed the food. When she had chewed the last bite of biscuit, Winnie laid the napkin down and looked at Frank. "What does Preston know that I don't?"

The door creaked, sparing Frank for a few more seconds. Louise made her way in, leaning on a wobbly cane. "It's me." Toodles circled her but stayed away from the cane, giving her room to move.

Frank helped her to the nearest chair.

Six weeks had passed since Winnie's Sunday visit, days when the temperatures had seemed to drop lower by the hour, along with Louise's health. Winnie had asked after her several times, but Frank had given general answers. "Not so good" didn't paint as bleak a picture as his sister's paler-than-moonlight features or a grown woman who could hardly get out of bed on some mornings.

"What's wrong, Louise?" Winnie bypassed Frank for an explanation. "Is it asthma?"

Louise shook her head. "At least, that is not what makes me so sick. The doctor wondered if it was bronchitis, but it's chronic, never goes away." She started coughing and didn't stop for several minutes. "He thinks I may have emphysema. My lungs don't take in oxygen efficiently. He wants me to see a specialist in Boston, someone who has treated this disease before and has better treatments to offer." She coughed again.

"So you are going to Boston for a medical appointment?" Winnie looked from Frank to Louise, then back to Frank, as if looking for the answer in his face.

Frank shook his head. "The treatments will take a while. Dr. Landrum has leads for work for Pa at the hospital where his daughter works." He looked at his feet, wishing he didn't have to add the last part. "I probably can get a job there, too."

He dragged his eyes away from the floor and looked straight at Winnie. "I will be going with them. Of course."

Louise tapped her cane on the floor. "I have told him he doesn't need to sacrifice his—and your—dreams for me, but he doesn't pay attention." In spite of her brave words, pain haunted her eyes and begged him to stay with her. He couldn't ignore her any more than he could drive past a man with a flat tire on the side of the road.

Winnie's dark eyes were pools of compassion, the same as he had seen when she served people at the soup kitchen. Moving next to Louise, she put her arm around her friend. "I haven't been a good friend, not a good friend at all."

Frank saw Winnie's tear-streaked face over his sister's shoulder. He could only watch and wonder at the friendship and love between these two women. Would Louise indeed flourish away from the community that had helped raise her?

Later, much later, Mom and Winnie helped Louise back to bed. When they didn't return, Frank went in search of them. He found them in his room, Mom going through the pile of things he meant to give away.

Winnie looked up when he entered. Clasping his championship medal in one hand, she dangled it between them.

"You want to leave this behind?"

Chapter 14

Lantern light brought out the golden highlights of Frank's medal as Winnie held it between them. At the moment, it looked as bright, as shiny, as extraordinary as it must have looked hanging around his neck almost five years ago. Gold, the color against which all other colors faded in comparison, even the still-treasured silver and bronze.

To think that Frank wanted to leave it behind. Give it away, in fact.

"If you want it, you can have it." He turned his back on her and walked out of the room. Mrs. Sawtelle looked at him, and then at Winnie, as if urging her to argue her son out of his foul mood. She followed him to the stairs. "Frank."

The single word was command and entreaty, all in one. Frank stopped, his back ramrod straight, stiff and unyielding. "It's the past, Winnie." He took a step down.

Winnie squeezed past him in the stairwell, planting one hand on the railing and the other on the wall. "But it's your past and one you should be proud of." She couldn't let him leave like this, defeat written in the slump of his shoulders, life drained from his face.

When she leaned forward to drape the medal around his neck, he caught her hand. "That thing brought short-term glory but it didn't help me keep a job and it hasn't helped Louise get better. It might as well be wood, hay or stubble that burn, instead of gold."

She searched his face. Where had the man gone who had worked by her side for the past three-and-a-half months? Where was the man who had convinced the children from the soup kitchen to sacrifice so that she could have a new pair of skates? Where had her dancing and skating partner gone?

Suddenly angry, she said, "I thought I could depend on you. I thought you believed in me. Of course, you have to help Louise. But this—" She slapped the medal into his hand. "This isn't about Louise. It's about you and me and our love of figure skating. You're throwing away something I hold very precious. You're not the man I thought you were."

With that, she turned her back on Frank and made it down the stairs and out the door without falling. She didn't stop running until she was halfway home. Coming to a stop, she studied the ground beneath her feet. She wanted to head to the mill and skate until her legs collapsed from exhaustion and her insides smiled from the effort. But if she planned to get to the church in time for the midmorning meal, she had to leave now. Her run now purposeful, her steps determined, she started reciting verses she had learned at the Seminary over the years in preparation for the annual scripture memory competition.

Her lips curved when she thought of the way her sister-in-law, Mary Anne, had surprised the community by winning both the memory portion and the Bible reading contest her first year in the community. Her brother, Wallace, had found his helpmate, something none of them expected when the blonde flapper had had an accident on the old bridge.

Winnie didn't have her sister-in-law's prodigious memory, but she retained a few favorite passages. She began with the first verse of Hebrews 11. "'Now faith is the substance of things hoped for, the evidence of things not seen.'"

Frank's medal gave her that evidence, proof that a person with talent, skill and hard work could make it to the top of the figure skating world. He had achieved everything she hoped for—at least at Nationals, and he would have gone further if not for the accident.

Faith played a role in Frank's achievement, a victory of spirit and determination. A victory that she believed God wanted her to win, as well. And Frank was throwing the medal away, as if it meant nothing.

Drawing in a deep breath of brisk fall air, she kicked the leaves piled on the ground. Dry and brittle, they flew at the touch of her boots. Of course Frank had to take care of Louise. She was disappointed that he was leaving, but that wasn't what made her mad.

No, her anger stemmed from the fact that he was leaving without telling her. If she hadn't showed up at his doorstep that morning, when would she have learned about his departure?

To herself, she could admit, she was more than angry. She also hurt in her soul. In discarding his medal, he was saying that her dreams, her hopes, meant nothing to him. To think she had fancied that he might have feelings toward her.

She dashed at the tears that threatened to start all over again. So what if he wasn't the man she'd thought he was? Women had survived much worse. Look at Danielle Parnell at the soup kitchen. She had let slip the fact that her husband had killed himself after she told him she was expecting another baby.

Frank wasn't worth her tears.

Louise poked her head into Frank's room.

"Go away."

Ignoring him, she tapped her way forward with the cane she used because she couldn't breathe well enough to walk very far. With a huff, she settled on his single chair.

"You shouldn't come with us. You belong here, with Winnie." She knocked her cane against the floor for emphasis.

"You think I haven't considered that?" Everyone in his family had tiptoed around him all week. He was glad Louise had finally brought it out in the open.

"You broke her heart. It's up to you to do something about it."

Frank wanted to punch something. Winnie Tuttle was the best thing that had happened to him since he came home in July, and he had treated her badly. He knew it, his family knew it, the Lord knew it, Nash had hounded him about it—and worst of all, Winnie felt rejected.

"You can't leave here with things like this. You have to go to her. Be a man, Frank. Go after her."

Too thin, taking a breath after every sentence, Louise was as determined a field commander as Green Mountain leader Ethan Allen had been. Frank knew he didn't stand a chance.

"Very well." He rolled his shoulders, seeking to ease the tension building in his muscles, before standing. "I will go, to get you off my back."

"Good." Louise's thin lips lifted in a satisfied smile. "Go on, then. I'll see you when you get back."

Grabbing his jacket, Frank bounded down the stairs two

at a time and burst out the door. He jogged by the fenced-in fields, empty now, the fall's crop making a small dent on the mortgage payment. His family had lived on this farm since his great-grandparents moved here from Canada at about the same time Winnie's grandmother was founding the Maple Notch Female Seminary, back in the 1860s.

He reached the last post and looked across the black dirt, imagining life without the farm, without Maple Notch, to return to. News reports indicated this kind of thing was happening all across the country. What would America be like in ten years, with people being uprooted and moved across the landscape like tumbleweeds?

Only God knew what the future held for any of them. Turning his back on the land, Frank headed for the Finch farmhouse and Winnie.

Down the road ahead of him, almost to the bridge, he saw her. She was heading to the soup kitchen as usual. "Winnie."

She stopped in her tracks and slowly turned around. "Frank."

He swallowed, his mouth suddenly dry. "Can we talk?"

"As long as we continue walking while we talk." He jogged to join her at the entrance to the bridge.

The shadows engulfed them under the roof, but Winnie didn't slow down.

Now that the time had come to talk, he didn't know how to start.

She decided for him. "How could you, Frank? How could you decide to leave Maple Notch and not even tell me?" She stopped walking.

What irony. She'd halted their forward progress in front of the courting plank, the one where some day Winnie and her future husband would probably carve their initials. Where he had dreamed of carving their initials, the swirling shapes of F and S with the strong lines of W and T.

Not that that would ever happen, not now. "I asked Nash—"

"Preston." The *S* in his name came out with a hiss. "That's fine and good. But were you too much of a coward to tell me yourself?" Her voice held a hint of hysteria, tears ready to flood her eyes and choke her words.

"Winnie." He put out a hand to touch her shoulder, but she brushed it off. "I promised myself I would see you before we left. I'm sorry I didn't come earlier, that I didn't come and tell you as soon as we made the decision. I just thought that with the problems Clarinda was having…" His voice trailed away. "No, that's an excuse. I was imitating an ostrich, I guess. Hoping some marvelous solution would be found, and I wouldn't have to leave."

Winnie didn't respond, and his shoulders heaved. "There is nothing I would like better than to stay here in Maple Notch. If we could spend eight hours a day training, I would be the happiest man on earth." Leaning forward, he wanted to meet those sweet lips with his own, but he caught himself in time. "It's my responsibility to help my family. To help Louise. They say they can get me a job, Winnie. I have to try."

She stood there, head turned away, foot tapping the road beneath her feet. "Didn't you think I would understand all of that?"

"I guess." He shrugged. "I don't know. I promise I'll keep in touch. I will pray for you every day. Nash is a good trainer. He got me ready—he'll do well with you."

"I know." Sniffling, Winnie ran a finger under her nose. "I dreamed of working with you. Since you're leaving, I feel like Santa Claus came back and took away my favorite Christmas present. With everything else that has happened, I can't help wondering if I'm wrong to keep going."

Before she finished speaking, he shook his head. "Absolutely not. You are gifted. You're so beautiful on ice, you take my breath away."

"I thought you didn't care about skating, about me. You were throwing your medal away."

How to explain? "It has nothing to do with you. That medal doesn't make a difference today. I let skating define who I was for too long. I'll always love skating. But I've got to let it go and help my family. If I could stay here and help you and earn money, I would. In a heartbeat."

"But you can't." Sighing, she wrapped her arms across her chest. "Did you mean what you said about my skating?"

"Every word."

"But you always tell me what I'm doing wrong."

"That's my job as your trainer." He grinned, something he never expected when he left this morning. "Even after the St. Louis Cardinals won the World Series, I expect manager Gabby Street had criticism of a play or two."

She rewarded him with a watery smile. "So, you will write? You promise?"

"I will. Cross my heart." He took her hands in his and kissed her knuckles. "You are destined for great things, Winifred Tuttle. Don't ever doubt that."

"You have mail." Alfred ran into the kitchen and dangled an envelope in front of Winnie. Heart pounding, she restrained herself from grabbing it out of her nephew's hand.

"It's postmarked from Boston." He peered at the upper right-hand corner as if struggling to make out the handwriting.

Clarinda took the envelope from her son and handed it to Winnie. "Mail is private, not to be opened by someone else upon penalty of the federal government." She winked at her sister. "Go ahead and read it in the privacy of your room."

"I'll do that." She stared at the address, the bold slashes of ink showing the strength in his fingers. The envelope banged against her hand as she dashed upstairs. Finding a ruler in the desk drawer, she used it in place of a letter opener. Several pages cascaded onto the floor.

His words jumped off the page as she bent over to pick them up. "…the job didn't pan out."

Winnie sank onto to the bed and buried her face in her hands.

Chapter 15

"Take care of yourself, Winnie." Danielle Parnell gave Winnie a brief hug as they closed the door to the church basement behind them on a crisp November day. "You've been looking right peaked these past few weeks. We can get by without you for a few days."

If only a warm meal and a quick nap would improve Winnie's spirits. She hadn't felt well since Frank had driven away, a little over three weeks ago.

Danielle walked with Winnie as far as the Seminary. She had found a room as well as a job helping out in the kitchen. In spite of the cramped quarters for a woman with two small children, she delighted in the work, and the children were the darlings of the students. "Are you continuing with your training? Every day?" she asked.

Her question surprised Winnie. "Every day." Her smile thinned. She went at the same time each day, and Preston took her through her routine step-by-step, inch by inch, analyzing, criticizing, sharpening, advising, encouraging.

Those skating questions took up a lot of space in her correspondence with Frank.

Oh, how she missed him. She missed skating with him, when he showed her how it was done. She pined for his laughter, his spirit, his core of courage. Every letter encouraged her to press forward, not to let his departure deter her from her goal. Next month began the competitions that would determine who would ultimately go to Nationals…and beyond.

"I was thinking I might come out and watch you one morning," Danielle said. "Perhaps another smiling face would encourage you to keep going."

Pleased by Danielle's offer, Winnie hugged her tight. "I'd love that! You can take the part of the cheering crowds. Or, of course, you could hold up a scorecard with a perfect six for my score. Just no boos, please."

Danielle smiled at that. "I'll come next week, then, after Thanksgiving." She turned in at the Seminary, and Winnie traveled on home.

That night, she joined Clarinda in the kitchen to bake several pies for Thursday. Anita slept in a cradle at Clarinda's feet, tucked beneath a blanket near the oven, where she would stay warm. Betty worked on crimping the crust with a fork and then rolling the cinnamon twirls Clarinda made out of the leftover crust. Norma's "help" consisted of dipping her spoon into the blueberry filling canned last summer and dipping apple slices in cinnamon sugar before eating the sweets.

"At least she doesn't like mincemeat or squash." Clarinda grinned as the girls dove after the cinnamon twirls hot out of the oven. "Now leave some for the boys. They like them too."

Betty pouted. "But they didn't help."

Clarinda put the remaining twirls out of reach on top of the refrigerator and set the pies to cool on the windowsill over the sink. When Howard came in, Winnie took over meal preparation so that he could have a few minutes alone with Clarinda. Five children didn't give them a lot of privacy.

The boys scarfed down the cinnamon-sugar treats in a minute, making Winnie glad they had baked a batch of sugar cookies to appease the after-dinner demands. Otherwise, they would whine for the pies. Behind closed doors, voices were raised in a fierce discussion, but Howard and Clarinda seemed peaceable when they came out for dinner.

After the meal, Howard gathered the family in the living room to continue reading *Leatherstocking Tales* by James Fennimore Cooper, one of the boys' favorites. He kept them up a little later than usual, taking them to the end of the book before closing the book with the words "the end."

"That one's good." Alfred leaned forward, pretending he was aiming a rifle. "Can we read it again?"

"I want to read about Pooh-Bear again," Norma said.

"We'll see." Howard put the book on the shelf and planted his hands on his knees. "Uncle Wallace and I are taking a trip. We're leaving in the morning."

"Will you be home in time for Thanksgiving?" Norma buried her head against his shoulder.

Howard looked at Clarinda, who was rocking in her chair and feeding Anita as the cat's tail swished in and out of harm's way. "Yes, he will. He'll only be gone for a night or two," she said.

Possibilities raced through Winnie's mind, but neither one of them elaborated further on the reason for the trip.

Personally, she'd almost rather skip Thanksgiving this year. She'd have to work harder than usual to develop a proper of attitude by Thursday.

After the hoped-for job didn't materialize, Frank had taken to pounding the streets of Boston. Block by block, he had extended the area of his search with each passing day. The good news was that nearly every block had some form of business. Most of them barely survived, the Closed for Business signs on storefronts around them frightening any sane person.

After several weeks of searching, Frank hadn't found a job. Pa had the promised position at the hospital where Louise remained a patient. At night, Frank stretched out on a thin mattress next to the bed his parents shared. In the morning, he rolled it up and waited his turn in the community bathroom before heading out for another day of job hunting. Late in the afternoon, he joined Mom at the hospital. Louise was breathing better, thanks to some marvelous machines. Together they went home and made a meal of out of bread and bacon drippings or some such. Pa hoped to buy a chicken for a Thanksgiving luxury. The thought made his mouth water.

This Tuesday, wind drove a miserable mixture of sleet and rain into his coat, soaking his trouser legs and the thin soles of his shoes. He didn't dare get sick and risk making Louise worse, so he decided to head home and warm up with a cup of weak tea and change into dry clothes. Maybe a letter from Winnie would await him, and he could escape for a few minutes into a world where hope and light still seemed possible.

A Model T with license tags that had raised white letters against a green background sat in front of the house where his family rented a room. The implication of the plates didn't strike him until he had a foot on the bottom step. Those were Vermont tags, not the black and white of Massachusetts.

Hope struggled in his chest as he mounted the stairs. Mrs. Conley, the widow who had taken them in, opened the door before he had his key out. "Mr. Sawtelle, I'm so glad you came home out of this miserable weather. You have visitors today. Take off your things and join them in the parlor."

Frank hung his dripping coat and hat on the coat tree by the door and removed his shoes to avoid dirtying the floors. He heard his guests before he saw them, the low murmur of men's voices with inflections unique to Vermont. The measured cadence of Wallace's speech, the deeper tones of Howard's voice. *Winnie.* Joy and worry rushed into Frank's throat, cutting off his breath for a brief second.

Recovering, he rounded the corner to the parlor. Wallace stood and shook Frank's hand before they settled back in their chairs. "Mrs. Conley didn't think you would return until later. I'm glad you're here, because we have something to discuss with you. You'll want to talk it over with your family, but we need an answer by morning."

Howard smiled. "I promised the children I'd be home in time for the holiday, of course."

Mrs. Conley brought in a tray with cups and a carafe of coffee. "I'll leave you gentlemen to visit."

The men appeared to be in Boston on a mission. Loosening his tongue from where it had stuck to the roof of his mouth, Frank asked, "Is Winnie all right?"

Wallace cleared his throat. "That's why we're here. In spite of our opposition last summer, I have come to admire her determination to continue in spite of everything that happened. Mr. Nash says—you say—she has real talent."

"What he's saying is that we were wrong to oppose Winnie's training," Howard said. "I know I'm coming late to the party, but I admit it now." He shook his head. "She's a whirlwind. The way she still rises before dawn every day, putting in I don't know how many hours at the rink before she heads over to town, and then she comes home and takes over for Clarinda. It's time for us to give her a break, now that Anita's past the danger point. Winnie needs to concentrate on the upcoming competitions."

It's about time. "I'm glad to hear it. It will be easier for Winnie to work every day if she knows you support her." As happy as Frank was with their decision, he didn't see why they had come to Boston.

Howard looked out the side window, where the house next door loomed close through the rain-streaked glass. Another glance took in the room, reminding Frank of his first impressions. Crowded. Old without being homey. Mrs. Conley had had to make do without much in her wallet even before the Depression hit, and now boarders filled her house to the rafters. The house didn't have the clean, lived-in feeling of their farmhouses at all. City living had its advantages, but they were hard to find in a place like this.

After his slow survey of the surroundings, Howard looked straight at Frank. "We wanted to know if you'd be willing to come back to Maple Notch."

Frank had known the request was coming, just as he had known what his response must be. "I can't."

Howard raised a hand. "Please hear me out before you refuse. You would live with us, in Wallace's old room in the attic. We'll pay you a small amount—should have been paying you all along, for helping Winnie—and there's some things you could help out with around the farm, if you've a mind to. You won't get much, but you won't go hungry."

If he were gone and making money, he could send money for Louise's care and not put further strain on his parents' pocketbook. Frank wanted to say yes so badly he could cry, but he did have one question to ask.

"Does Winnie know about your plan?"

Wallace answered. "No. We didn't want to disappoint her, in case you can't come."

"And what a lovely Thanksgiving surprise it will be if

you show up at the door tomorrow night. Please say yes."
Howard came close to begging.

"I'll ask Mom and Pa when they get home, but…yes. I
want to come."

Chapter 16

"When is Daddy coming home?" Betty sat on the edge of her bed, her elbows resting on her knees, holding her head with her hands. "He *promised* he'd be back in time for Thanksgiving."

Winnie couldn't remember the last time Howard had been gone overnight, let alone for two nights. "I'm sure he'll be here before the big dinner tomorrow, I promise." She leaned over and kissed Betty, then Norma, before turning off the light and shutting the door behind her.

Precious girls. Would she have boys or girls, or would she ever get married at all? Once again her thoughts circled back to Frank. *Frank.* She sighed.

A car horn honked and Betty dashed out the door before Winnie could stop her. "Daddy's home!" She ran down the stairs, Norma following her, leaving Winnie at the top of the stairs. She decided to head to her room and let the children welcome their father home.

"Aunt Winnie!" Betty's voice called Winnie back before she reached her door. "You'd better get down here."

Winnie ran her hand along the stair rail, turning at the top stair and peering toward the front door.

"Hello, Winnie."

Frank Sawtelle grinned up at her.

Thanksgiving morning Winnie woke up at four o'clock, as if not a day had passed since Frank had left. Through the heating vent in her floor, she heard Clarinda's laughter and the low murmur of conversation. A glance at the clock confirmed the early hour. Clarinda had probably stayed up after Anita's last feeding to put the turkey in the oven, but who else was downstairs? A promising new day stretched out before her, now that Frank had returned. She pulled on her blue jeans and a lightweight sweater and headed downstairs.

When she slipped into the kitchen, she found Frank sitting at the table, tucking into a short stack of pancakes and a rasher of bacon as if he hadn't seen a hot breakfast for a while. He smiled when she came into the room. "Good. You're up." He pointed at her with an egg-yolk-coated fork. "We're going to the mill today."

Winnie accepted the plate Clarinda handed to her, her mouth watering at the smell of the hot maple syrup oozing over the pancakes. She couldn't remember the last time she had eaten anything besides oatmeal for breakfast. "I can't believe you went to all this trouble, with the big meal at noon. Speaking of which—" She sat down and took a bite of the pancakes, moist with pumpkin and spiced with cinnamon and nutmeg, before continuing. "As much as I want to run to the ice and spend the day there, I need to stay home today. This morning, at least, to help with the children and the cooking."

"Nonsense." Clarinda joined them at the table with her

own plate of food. "Howard didn't drive all the way to Boston and back for you to spend the morning listening to the radio announcer describe the Felix the Cat balloon in the Macy's parade and stick a spoon in a pot once in a while. You and Frank go over there to the ice. I've already talked with Mr. Nash. He's expecting you, and then you make sure he comes back here and eats with us."

The only thing that might make the day better was a cup of hot cocoa with some whipped cream on top, or a peppermint stick.

"Are you going to stare at the food all day?" Frank pushed away from the table and carried his plate to the sink. "Thanks so much, Mrs. Finch."

Clarinda pushed a curl away from her forehead. "Oh, please, call me Clarinda." She reached behind her for the Bible she kept on the telephone stand. "While Winnie finishes eating, I'd appreciate it if you read from Psalm 136. That always comes to mind for me on Thanksgiving."

Winnie silently mouthed the echoing refrain, *for his mercy endureth forever.* By the time he finished the psalm—twenty-six repetitions later—Winnie had cleaned her plate. "Let me grab my skates and I'm ready."

Doubly grateful now that she had dressed in comfortable clothes for the morning, Winnie joined Frank in a slow jog through the fields. "I see you've continued working out."

"Yes." She kept her answer short, not wanting to complain about either Preston or Frank's absence.

"But?"

"You'll see." She hoped he wouldn't tear her routine apart too badly. Sloppy, that's how she was skating these days, and he wouldn't stand for it.

All the questions that Winnie wanted to ask sat on the tip of her tongue, begging for a voice, but she didn't dare.

Louise was still sick, and Winnie had expected him to stay in Boston until she improved or until…well…the end came.

Answers could wait until later. Frank was back in time for a final push to get ready for the all-Vermont competition (which she had won the past two years) in December, the all–New England competition, which she won in a surprise showing last year, and then…Nationals. And even, God willing, the next level.

The winter games opened in Lake Placid in three and a half months. How could she possibly hope to compete?

Preston met them at the door with a smile. The handshake between the two men was as warm as a hug. Within minutes, Frank stepped onto the ice, but Winnie hesitated at the gate, suddenly shy. Today she was almost more nervous than she had been the first time they had shared the ice. She waited a moment, praying for renewed faith in the possible victory that lay ahead.

Frank glided onto the ice, expecting Winnie to follow. When she didn't, he circled back to the gate. "I'm eager to see the progress you've made on your routine, but you have to do the usual warm-ups. The last thing you need is to pull a muscle."

Stretching and skating, footwork and spins. If possible, he had forgotten how beautiful she looked on the ice.

For a while, he joined her in the exercises, and then he retired to the end of the ice. "I want you to go through everything. Your figures. The free skate. I'll be watching, taking notes, deciding where we need to focus our efforts." He knew he was brusque—he meant to be. For all the beauty on the ice, the figure skating world was not a gentle arena. The tenderhearted Winnie might wilt under the force of their criticism. More than ever, he had to distance himself from her emotionally if he wanted her to reach her potential.

Her figures were barely acceptable. They might have to work harder than either one of them imagined possible to even get back to Nationals. She looked at him, a worried expression on her face, as if she knew how poor her performance had been. He schooled his face into neutrality. At the side of the room, Nash turned on the gramophone to play "Climb a Tree with Me."

Now Frank struggled to keep the smile that was leaping inside his heart from his face. She was poetry on ice. As she worked her way down the ice, doing the required footwork during the instrumental solo of the song, she looked as beautiful as Odette in *Swan Lake.*

Then and there, he knew she could make it all the way.

After the last note, she turned to him, face alight as if anticipating approval. He refused to give it. To be honest with himself, he would have to watch it again, to pay attention to her feet and legs, and the height of the jumps. He doubted it was as perfect as it seemed.

She skated the length of the ice toward him. "I know I singled that double axel."

She had? He knew the routine as well as she did, but he hadn't noticed her mistakes. He simply nodded. "We'll talk about it later. Now go out there and go through the figures."

The look she gave him could have cut the ice more efficiently than a skate blade, but she did as instructed. He kept his attention focused enough to see that her figure eights still lacked precision. If she didn't get that under control, she could miss the top spot at the bigger competitions. At least she needed him for something. He didn't want to receive pay without offering value in return. His only reason—at least the only *valid* reason—for accepting money in the first place was to help his family.

After the figures, her shoulders sagged as she skated toward him. Frank wondered what to do next when Nash called from overhead. "Anyone want some hot cocoa?"

"Sure, we need a break." Frank accepted for both of them.

"You read my mind." Winnie raced from the ice and stripped off her skates quicker than Frank had ever seen, beating him up the stairs. Halfway down the hall, she stumbled and cried out.

"What's wrong?" Frank rushed to her side, but she shook her foot with ease. When she took a step, though, she winced. She bent over and studied the toe of her sock. "I got a splinter. Preston's got a pair of tweezers in his office."

Moments later, Winnie sat on the folding chair, a cup of cocoa resting on Nash's desk, her right foot resting on a chair in front of her while she leaned over, looking at it from side to side. "I can't find it. It must be on the bottom of my foot."

"Let me look." Frank knelt in front of her, holding her foot in his hands. Old scars appeared in her flesh, and her ankles were black and blue from bruises. Her toenails were short, but painted with a light pink color. She noticed him looking at them and blushed. "The girls like to paint my nails."

The girls. Many times he had seen Winnie with her nieces and nephews. She would make a good mother someday. *Don't think about it. Stick to business.*

He ran his fingers over the soles of her feet, and she wiggled. "That tickles."

"There it is." He pressed harder and she grimaced as the sliver of wood pushed its way through her skin. He pulled it out and discarded it in the basket by Nash's desk. Her feet were calloused, hardened from her hours on the ice. "Do you have any salve I can put on her feet?"

"Happens I do." Nash opened the bottom drawer to his desk and pulled out a tin Frank had seen before, one that claimed the contents were as good for human skin as for the cow's udders, where it was applied during cold weather.

Frank rubbed it between his fingers then worked on

the soles of Winnie's feet, starting with the one that had the splinter.

"What are you doing?" Winnie's feet wiggled, but he kept applying pressure.

Taking care of you. "Taking care of your feet. You can't avoid the bumps and bruises, but you can do something about dry and broken skin. Do this, every day, at home. Howard must have something like this he uses with the cows. Ask if you can borrow it."

Kneeling there, massaging her feet, Frank looked up into her sparkling brown eyes and wished he had a ring box in his hand, and held her hands instead of her feet. He wanted to lean forward, to claim those lips for a kiss. Instead, he shut the lid on the can, wiped his hands, slid her socks onto her feet and stood. "It's time I go earn my keep."

Confusion replaced the sparkle in Winnie's eye. "What do you mean, earn your keep?"

Frank straightened while he considered his answer. They hadn't asked him to keep it a secret. "Wallace and Howard are paying me a salary so I can focus on working with you."

Anger flashed in her eyes. "You mean, you're doing this for money?"

Chapter 17

After Winnie woke on Saturday morning, she yawned and stretched before climbing out of bed. Today she would enjoy a brief break from the torture of training that had dominated her world from dawn until dusk and sometimes late into the evening since Frank's return ten days ago.

He was making sure her family got their money's worth. She had allowed herself to think he had returned to Vermont out of a deep concern for her, and instead he came for a perfectly acceptable reason that had no romance attached to it. He needed money, and they had offered him a job.

That explained why he barked orders and found fault with every millimeter of movement across the ice.

But today they were holding a skating party for the children. She had arranged for Preston to serve hot cocoa with candy canes. Danielle had offered to serve the food and corral the children. She had even agreed to let Eugene try skating.

Winnie enjoyed watching children who had only begun

to walk try their luck on the slippery surface. Her nephew Carl would be skating today, too, for only the second time.

By the time the two boys reached Norma's age of three, they would be seasoned skaters. Winnie grinned at the thought. Norma might be able to outskate her brothers in a few years. Maybe not, though. Howie had a competitive streak that wouldn't be denied.

A rapping at her door was followed by, "Are you ready?" *Frank*. Her prison guard, or guardian of her future, depending on what mood she was in.

"Coming." She slipped on her sweater and headed out the door. He joined her every day for oatmeal and coffee. "There's snow on the ground this morning. Dress warm."

Winnie almost wished they could ride in a car, to avoid the icy walk that could end her career with a single misstep. But even if they wanted to waste money on gas, the shortest route to the mill lay over the fields. Most winter days, her feet found the path by memory, trampling the snow into the same footpath she had worn through the grass over the course of the years.

Fortified by hot oatmeal and coffee, she pulled her boots over her socks, buttoned up her coat, lifted the collar so that it covered her neck and tied her scarf so that it covered her face up to her nose. Last of all, she pulled on mittens.

Frank laughed when he saw her outfit. "We're just headed to the mill, not to the North Pole."

"I heard the wind blowing outside. Wait till you see me in January."

Long icicles hung from the eaves of the house. Winnie remembered how she used to break them off to suck on. Adults always said the icicle would make her feel colder but she didn't care, as long as she could run inside and get warm again. She had never complained about being cold on the ice. She would skate outside year round if the surface stayed hard enough.

Hands stuffed in his pockets, Frank hunched over as he walked. Light bounced off the tree branches, encased as they were in ice and snow, and they hung lower than usual under the weight. Winnie dodged a branch, but Frank wasn't so lucky. He caught it with his shoulder, and it showered snow on them both.

Frank stuttered forward a couple of steps and shook himself free of the snow. Winnie giggled as she shook snow off herself, as well. Picking a clump of snow off her coat, she tossed it at Frank.

"So that's the way it is." Bending over, he came up with two handfuls he tossed in her direction. Soon snow flew through the air, both of them bending and dodging.

When they stopped, Winnie laughed, and Frank was relaxed. But they had delayed the start of practice long enough. All work and no play…Winnie sighed. She had pleaded and pouted and made everyone around her miserable until they found a way to make her dream happen. She wouldn't dishonor their sacrifice—or her dream—for anything short of an emergency.

Frank's friendly demeanor proved to be short-lived. He glanced at the clock upon their arrival and frowned. "We'd better get busy. We'll be losing time later today when the kids arrive, and we're getting off to a late start."

To listen to him, one would think he planned practice down to the last second. Perhaps he did. She exchanged her boots for skates and headed for the ice while he hunched over, staring at a piece of paper in his hands. She knew it consisted of notes he had made from their practice the day before. He always found something to correct. On the rare occasions when he didn't, he told her that one day did not a medal win; she had do it consistently, every day.

The snow play remained the high point of the day as they worked through her free-skate routine, move by move.

The first time through, she two-footed the landing on the toe loop.

He stopped her. "Start over."

On the second try, she popped out of a double jump that became a single. She stopped and began again. Time after time she made mistakes. It turned into her worst start of the week, and she was close to tears before he called a halt.

Skating a final lap to shake the stress and unhappiness from her legs before she called it quits, she glanced out the windows. The church wagon trundled down the road, children lined up along the sides, pointing at the mill. The picture brought a smile to her face. If children couldn't cheer her up, she was hopeless.

By the time she had her shoes back on, the wagon had arrived. Preston held the door open as the guests came in. Winnie watched for Danielle, hoping her friend hadn't changed her mind at the last minute about coming.

"Oh, here she is." Danielle walked forward, Olive in her arms and Eugene holding her hand.

Frank stared at her and stiffened without speaking.

"Hello, Frank. I bet you weren't expecting to see me."

Frank thought he was prepared for anything until Danielle Parnell walked through the door of the rink. A cold ball in the pit of his stomach had unraveled over the course of the past few months, but now it seized up, freezing emotions and disappointment in place. "Hello, Danielle."

Winnie looked from one to the other, confusion clear on her features. "You two know each other?"

What was Danielle doing in Maple Notch? "Welcome to the ice. I thought you had retired."

She nodded. "Winnie insisted I bring Eugene, that he was just the right age to start skating. I couldn't deny him the opportunity."

Frank had seen the children. "When...who?" He stopped

himself before he pried further. "You can tell me about it later." He turned to Winnie. "Why didn't you tell me you knew Danielle?"

Winnie looked confused. "She never mentioned you." She turned to Danielle. "You knew I was working with Frank. Why didn't you tell me you knew him?"

Danielle glanced around. "People are coming in. Can we talk about this later?"

By the expression on her face, Winnie wanted to let go of this conversation about as much as a dog wanted to let go of a bone with meat still on it. "It does appear we're gathering a crowd, and you probably don't want everyone to know your business."

Frank counted the people in the crowd. A little larger than the numbers in the summer—Winnie had warned him about that. One of the boys ran up to him. "Remember me?"

How could he forget? "You're Johnny. Where's your sister?"

"Over there." He nodded toward a gaggle of girls, giggling over something. Frank liked hearing their laughter, a sign that childhood joy remained in this place.

Soon the children were on the ice. "We'll give them a chance to warm up before we hold races. They're all excited to try again. We have peppermint drops for everyone today." Winnie grinned. "Why don't I hold Olive while the two of you go on the ice with Eugene?"

Frank hid his grin as Winnie handed Danielle a pair of skates, and she tugged boots onto Eugene's feet. Before they knew it, they were on the ice. Both Frank and Danielle reached down for one of Eugene's hands. When the skates slipped beneath the little boy's feet, he looked up, panic in his eyes. "It's okay. It's a different kind of walking." Frank scooted one foot forward first, then the other.

Danielle looked down at the boy. "Go ahead. Try."

He did and wobbled as his right foot moved, but he remained upright. Then he brought his right foot forward, and he looked up, triumph written on his features.

"Well done! He's a natural skater, but no surprise there." Frank grinned at Danielle. "When did you get married?"

She shook her head. "It was no one you knew. He represented a company that sponsored one of the competitions I entered, after you retired. We had a whirlwind romance. Before I knew what had happened, I was married and had a baby."

So where was the man now? Frank knew of cases where men abandoned their families, unwilling to face a future without the wealth they had come to depend on. But she had another baby....

A sad smile crossed her face. "Gene tried, he truly did. He used what wealth his family had to keep the company going, to provide for the men and families who depended on them. But the money would only stretch so far. And when he learned I was pregnant again, he took me back to my parents before—before he took the coward's way out."

She continued her story as they worked their way around the edges of the rink, the older children whizzing by. Her parents lost their home and moved into their son's house; they didn't have room for Danielle and her children. "I wandered for a while. When I came to Maple Notch, I remembered how you talked so much of the kindness here, and I experienced it myself at the soup kitchen. I met Winnie that first day. By the time I realized she knew you and all of that, I was too embarrassed to introduce myself."

"Until today."

"Yes. Although I still haven't told her about my own skating career. I will, though."

Frank wondered at the peaceful expression on Danielle's face. After she had left skating for marriage and children, it seemed her dreams had crashed as surely as his had.

"Winnie has been a good friend. She helped me to stop feeling sorry for myself and start believing in God's goodness again," Danielle said.

Frank grunted. "She tends to have that effect on people."

"On you, too?" She looked sideways at him.

"Sometimes."

"And you on her, I think. Even if you do it by being hard on her."

"Is that what she says?"

Eugene fell down. "I tired, Mommy." He lifted his arms for Danielle to pick him up.

They didn't speak any more until they reached the gate. Winnie sat on the bench, bouncing the baby and playing a game of pat-a-cake with her. She looked up with a smile, and the baby reached for her mother. Danielle sank onto the bench next to Winnie, shifted Eugene to one knee while taking the girl on her other. "I should have told you this a long time ago, Winnie. I knew Frank when he competed at Nationals. I was there three times myself, although I never won top place."

Winnie's face flashed through a dozen expressions. "You're *that* Danielle? Danielle Duncan, from Connecticut?"

"One and the same," Frank said, placing a hand on Danielle's shoulder, and she turned a pale pink.

Chapter 18

A week after the skating party, Winnie arrived at the ice skating arena in Bennington for the second day of the all-Vermont competition. After yesterday's school figures, today she would compete in the free skate.

Frank, Preston and Danielle had made the trip with her. Clarinda had offered to keep Danielle's children for the day.

Butterflies fluttered in Winnie's stomach, and Danielle squeezed her hand. "Don't worry. Your routine last week, when Frank made you perform in front of all of us without any warning, was outstanding. You'll do fine."

Winnie smiled. "I hope so. I'm not really worried. It's my third year in the adult division, and I won before." In spite of her confident words, her insides told a different story. She could almost hear the whispers. *She's the reigning champion. She won the past two years. She even went to Nationals last year.*

Danielle must know how she was feeling. Winnie said,

"I can't believe you never told me you used to compete. That you met Frank at his first all–New England competition."

Danielle laughed. "I used to do a lot of things that I don't do any more. Danielle Parnell, alone with two small children, isn't the same person as the woman who used to figure skate."

"I don't know about that." Winnie squeezed her hand. At the table, the woman taking registrations had engaged Frank in conversation. In spite of the smile on Frank's face, Winnie hoped he didn't find the day difficult. When she had asked him to help her, she hadn't considered the burden that returning to an arena he had once dominated might place upon him. She hadn't thought of a lot of things.

Preston returned before Frank did. "You're in the final set. That's to be expected, of course." He nodded as a couple of men passed by.

"Good luck, Miss Tuttle. I'm cheering you on." A young girl waved, and Winnie remembered seeing her last year. She showed a lot of promise.

"No one knows me here," Danielle said. "I don't know if I'm brave enough to go to all–New England."

"Assuming I get there." Winnie sent up a brief prayer. She had to win at all–New England, or at least place high enough to go to Nationals, to have any hope of going further. What if she didn't even get out of Vermont? What if…?

Frank appeared at her elbow. "Come here. You need a good dose of hot cocoa."

"How about some coffee?" Winnie asked.

This time Danielle laughed. "You need sugar with the caffeine. Trust me."

With three friends hemming her in, Winnie couldn't pace as she often did. They took her through the cafeteria line early, watched what she ate, made sure she had plenty to drink, then marched with her to the waiting area. At the door, Danielle gave her a goodbye hug. "Only coaches are allowed in here. I'll see you later, after you win."

"Good luck." Preston clamped his hand on her shoulder, then disappeared.

"It's just you and me, then." Winnie looked into Frank's greener-than-usual eyes.

"You'll do fine. I know it." He brought his hands together in what might have been a clap and rubbed them. "Don't worry about yesterday's scores. You should win here."

With those not-so-encouraging words, he had her run in place. "We didn't get our usual morning run in." He moved his legs up and down, joining her in the exercise.

After they finished the stretches, she asked, "Shall we dance? That's what we usually do when we can't get on the ice."

With a smile, he took her in his embrace and waltzed her around the floor. She giggled, unable to stop herself.

"We'd better stop making a scene." Frank smiled as they stepped apart.

The coordinator walked into the room. "You're up." The time had arrived to warm up on the ice before Winnie's group skated.

Frank laid his hands on her shoulders. "I would tell you to break a leg, except that you're not an actor. So let's say a prayer instead." Taking her hands in his, he said quietly, so only the two of them and the Almighty could hear, "Lord, Winnie has worked and prepared for this moment. May she skate as she has rehearsed, and to You be the glory."

"Amen."

On the ice, a cheering crowd greeted Winnie, and her heart swelled with confidence. Here she was known and loved. After waving, she blocked out the audience and went through a series of jumps and spins that she couldn't do on the hardwood floor of the waiting room.

The bell rang, and Winnie left the ice feeling much more confident. Back in the waiting room, Frank frowned as he studied a sheet of paper.

"What's the problem?" Tension threatened to return. She peeked over his shoulder; he held the score sheet from yesterday's compulsory figures.

"You didn't do quite as well as I had hoped. You have a little more room to make up than I expected."

A shiver passed over Winnie. "I will do my best."

Waiting while everyone else skated was the hardest part. Five women skated ahead of her in the final group. One of them was competing at the senior level for the first time, and Winnie didn't consider her a threat, at least, not this year. The woman who won the silver medal a year ago came in, face wreathed in smiles and bragging about scores in the high fives. Winnie tapped the toe of her skate guard against the floor.

The coordinator poked her nose into the room. "Winifred Tuttle. You're next."

Frank's smile was the last thing Winnie saw as she headed for the door. Unless she counted the surprise performance Frank had sprung on her at last week's party, this was the first time she would perform her "Climb a Tree with Me" routine for an audience. She put herself in position, arms raised above her head, poised for the first note.

By the time she made it through her double Lutz/double toe loop combination jump, she knew she was skating well. She floated through the remainder of the routine. On the final note, she held her camel sit spin one last second before straightening and bowing. Frank waited for her in the spot where coach and skater together received the judge's scores. *Three perfect sixes and two five-point-nines.* Her hand flew to her throat.

Before she knew it, she was at the top of the medal stand, accepting the gold medal. She had crossed her first barrier to reach Nationals.

Frank stood by the Christmas tree, his hand touching the star ornament at the top. He had placed the same crooked star at the top since he was a little boy. Pa used to lift him in the air so he could reach the topmost branch. He had cut a tree from their farm and brought it to Boston tied to the top of the car when he drove in yesterday. Otherwise, he doubted if his parents would have bothered with a tree, not in their crowded room. It ended up in the community parlor, but with their family ornaments. He brought a couple of boxes from the house, looking for a way to make this Christmas away from home a little more familiar.

"So, Winnie is all set for the all–New England competition in two weeks." Louise smiled from her spot by the fire. The doctors had agreed for her to spend a couple of hours at home on Christmas day, provided she went back before nightfall. Her improved health was all the Christmas present the family wished for.

"Winnie was amazing," Frank said. There should have been scores higher than a six for the way she skated last Saturday. She deserved every glint of light off the gold medal on her chest. It was, indeed, a glorious victory. He might have guided her, but the inner spark was all hers.

"I'm so happy for both of you." Louise remained as thin as ever, but her breathing seemed less labored, and her cheeks had a little more color. More than that, she had taken a renewed interest in life. "Are you sure there's nothing going on between you?"

"No."

"Then how about Danielle?"

Frank remembered when his parents thought, hoped,

something might develop between him and Danielle. "No. Even if I was interested—and I'm not—she isn't. She's been in Maple Notch for months and never came around. And I got the impression she's seeing someone in town."

"I'm not surprised. You cut off contact with everyone who cared about you after your accident." In spite of the light tone, Louise's words held censure.

"You're right." He studied the clusters of tinsel on the tree. "Do you remember the arguments we used to have about whether we should hang the tinsel on piece by piece, or to throw it on in clumps?"

The memory brought a smile to Louise's face. "You claimed that clumps were more realistic, because that's the way snow collects on trees."

"And you said it should be a single, long strand, because that was more like icicles. Like the ones hanging from the rafters."

"I still think that, every time I see an icicle out my window. Have you changed your mind?"

Frank lifted the clump from the tree and sorted out two or three single strands. "It goes further your way. We can spread it out more, instead of a handful of clumps."

"Last year we picked off as many as we could when we took down the tree. So we wouldn't need to buy more this year."

"I noticed." Frank had found the tinsel, carefully wrapped and laid on top of the other ornaments.

The door opened, and Pa came in. "Merry Christmas." He hung his coat on a hook before he hugged Frank. "It's good to see you, son." His job as a janitor at the hospital where Louise was a patient had him working on the holiday, but they were doubly grateful, for the income as well as for the reduced rate available to employees. He planted a gentle kiss on Louise's forehead. "They said if you do well today, you may get to leave the hospital soon."

"I feel so much better, Pa. Thank you for bringing me home."

He sat down next to Frank. "What shall we do while we wait for dinner?"

Frank had to smile. Pa never did wait very well, always on the move. The fact that he had survived in good spirits after a couple of months in the tight confines of the rented room surprised his son.

"Look what we have here." Louise pointed to a bookshelf next to her chair. "It's a jigsaw puzzle of a covered bridge! In fact—" she leaned in, studying the image "—I do believe it's the old bridge from Maple Notch."

Frank had it out quickly and found a card table. A wave of homesickness washed over him when he saw the familiar sight. "I wonder if they would let us keep it." He studied the details of the picture on the box lid, while Louise and Pa found the edge pieces. "It's too bad the old bridge is gone." He set the box down with a sigh and fitted two pieces together.

"You can still carve your initials on the new courting plank. Right up there beneath Wallace and Mary Anne's initials."

"Can't. That spot's already filled."

Louise giggled. "So you have thought about it."

Heat warmed his cheeks as if he were standing outside the fiery furnace Daniel wrote about. While Pa and Louise worked on the border, he fished for pieces of faded red, the color of the roof. Soon he had a picture emerging on his side of the table.

"I bet there's enough space left for a pair of initials, if you make them small." Louise practically whispered. "You've got to keep it in the family."

Frank didn't bother replying that time. His family had their minds made up.

At the end of the day, after he helped Pa return Louise to the hospital, his father stopped him from heading home. "How are things going between you and Winnie? Does your mother have reason to hope?"

"Pa, I can't. What do I have to offer her? In two months' time, I expect her to compete with the best skaters in the world. It's my job to get her there, that's all."

"Now, look here, son, I've known Winifred Tuttle all her life. Love her about as much as I love our Louise. You're a good man, and she knows it."

Frank shook his head. "I won't take her mind off the goal, not when gold is still within her reach."

Chapter 19

The calendar had turned to 1932, but instead of future dreams, Winnie's hopes lay shattered on the floor of the room where she was staying during the all–New England competition.

The alarm went off, reminding her she must get up. She should spend a long time soaking in a hot bath and do everything possible to prepare her bruised leg for a hard day's work.

Instead she pulled her blanket over her head and turned on her side, staring at the ice-coated window. No matter how much she wished she could blink this day away, her brain refused to sleep. She kept reliving the failure of yesterday's school figures, like a broken film reel.

A sharp rap sounded at the door. "Are you ready?" Frank was early.

"Go away."

"Either you come out or I'm coming in." Frank sounded determined enough to do it.

She might never skate at the all–New England competition again after today, but she couldn't let Frank catch her in her night clothes. "Coming." She pulled on her robe and opened the door a crack. "You're early. I'm not ready."

Frank lounged against the doorjamb as if he didn't have a single worry. "I didn't hear any sounds coming from your room. I figured I'd better make sure you were doing everything according to plan." He looked her up and down. "Which you're not. So get started. I'll be back in thirty minutes to take you to breakfast."

High-handed, but what did she expect? If he wouldn't allow himself to feel sorry when his student failed so miserably, of course he expected her to bounce back.

Twenty-nine minutes later exactly, Winnie opened the door as soon as Frank knocked. Her hair was still damp, but her costume called for her springing curls to fly free, so she wasn't concerned.

As they walked the hall, Frank whistled the old, familiar song—"Faith Is the Victory."

"Would you stop whistling?"

"What?"

Her question must have caught him off guard. "Whistling that song. There's no victory in store for me today."

"Is that what's bothering you?" They reached the dining hall, and he opened the door. "In case you didn't notice, you weren't the only one to take a fall yesterday."

She sniffed. "No matter what you say, I'm still in fifth place. Almost impossible to make up today, no matter how well I do."

"Nonsense. If you skate your free skate as well as I have seen you do it, you can win. No problem."

Once in the dining room, Frank signaled the waiter. He touched the top of Winnie's menu to get her attention. "I'm ordering for both of us."

"But it's all so expensive." The outrageous prices made

Winnie even more grateful for the hearty meals she ate three times a day. The cost of home-cooked meals couldn't compare. They could hardly afford to buy a bowl of cereal here at the hotel, let alone the kind of food she usually consumed on competition days. She should have remembered, after last year.

Frank patted her hand, as if to reassure her. "We'll each take a farmer's special, eggs over easy, dry toast, fresh orange juice and coffee if you have it."

The waiter disappeared, and Winnie glared at Frank. "We can't afford these prices."

He grabbed a biscuit from the basket on the table and buttered it. "You should know better. You're an athlete. You need to eat well, especially on competition days. Here, take a biscuit." He handed her the one he had buttered.

"My stomach gets too nervous to want to eat." She bit into the biscuit, and it slid down her throat easily. She took a second bite and swallowed some milk.

Frank nodded, as if satisfied. He didn't speak again until the waiter brought the food. A long, full, half hour later, Winnie had emptied her plate. "I can't believe I ate all that." She scooted over, ready to get out of the booth.

"Stay put." Frank asked the waiter for more coffee. After it had been poured, he took a sip.

"You're acting as if yesterday never happened." Winnie frowned at her coffee cup. "I can't stop thinking about it."

"Yes, you can. You *must.* This is what you have spent months preparing for, why you have gone through the routine thousands of times. You could skate it backward if you needed to."

She smiled at that. "I've never been so nervous before a competition." Her smile faded. "People have sacrificed so much to get me here. I feel like I failed them yesterday…I failed God…I failed *you.*"

His eyes melted into gray as he looked at her. "You

could never fail me. And I've heard skaters say that they worry if they're *not* nervous before a competition. That nerves give them the edge to do their best work. Otherwise, they're complacent. So—let's pray before we get started on the rest of the day."

After the prayer, they headed back to their rooms and Winnie brought out her skating costume. It was lovely, a cinnamon bodice with full skirt and beige accents, but she had never cared for it, and it certainly didn't fit the mood of the music she was skating to. A deep plum color would have, perhaps, to match the sentimentality of the words.

But she had worn the cinnamon-colored outfit before and there was no need to waste money on something new. The judges weren't worried about what she was wearing, but how she skated. She packed the costume into her bag, with her skates, to carry to the arena. Next, she sat in front of her mirror, brushing her hair in an attempt to bring order to the curls. They were a little more cooperative since her bath, and a tan headband would hold them in place while she skated.

Since the block to the arena was clear of snow, they walked to their destination. "Prepare yourself," Frank said.

As soon as they neared the building, a voice called out, "Smile, Miss Tuttle! Mr. Sawtelle!" A flashbulb went off in her face, and her arm automatically shot up.

"Relax," Frank whispered in her ear, remembering how intrusive reporters had seemed. "You're the return-ing champion. Act like one."

Whispers rustled around them, invading the cocoon he tried to create for them. *Who's that? He looks familiar. That's Frank Sawtelle. He won Nationals a few years back. How terrible to hear about that accident.*

Ignoring the whispers came more easily than Frank ex-pected. Smiling and waving, he felt a sense of homecoming. He belonged here, Winnie belonged, and she would do well. He believed it. "Imagine what the gauntlet will be like after you win today."

The red flooding Winnie's cheeks tickled him.

Her fifth-place finish in compulsories qualified her for the final group of the day in the free skate, and she would skate second. She would suffer agonies while watching the other four skaters seek to surpass her total score. In spite of his confident words, she did face a difficult challenge: put up a score that could withstand four attempts to outdo her. She would have to earn the highest scores of the day, higher than she had ever earned, but he knew she could. He knew she would.

To demonstrate his confidence in her win, he decided to act before they knew the outcome of today's competition. When she ducked into the changing room, he said, "I'll be back in a few minutes." He wandered down the hall in search of a skater he had seen yesterday: Sean Rafferty, a fellow medalist in 1927.

He spotted the cap of red hair as he made his way down the crowded hall. "Sean!"

Sean turned in search of the person calling his name, and Frank repeated his greeting. "Over here, Sean."

Sean bade goodbye to the people around him and greeted Frank with a firm handshake. "It's good to see you back, friend. Hear tell you're coaching the young Tuttle girl."

"We grew up as next-door neighbors."

"Oh, like that, is it? Come on, you look like a man with something serious on his mind." Sean led him in the direction of a coffee urn and poured a cup for both of them. "So. You decided to return."

Frank shrugged. "I still can't skate. At least not..." He swept the air with his arms. "Not in this environment. But when Winnie asked for my help, I couldn't say no."

"She had a tough day yesterday. If she wants to win." No judgment in the statement.

Frank nodded. "Yes. She's beating herself up for it pretty badly, but I am convinced she will make it back to Nationals. That's why I wanted to talk with you."

"So you didn't just want to see me for my good looks and charm?" Sean waved at someone as he went by. "Look, we're not going to get any privacy here. I'll get us into the men's waiting area. It should be empty."

Although Frank hadn't competed in this arena, he still experienced a sense of déjà vu as he encountered the odors, sounds and sights of the skating world he had dominated for a brief time.

"So, what do you need from me?" Sean asked.

"We need a place to stay during Nationals. We stayed at a hotel last night, but we can't afford the prices in New York. Then I remembered that you made your home in the city."

"Sure, my wife would love to have company. Even if all we do is talk about figure skating." His friend leaned his back against the wall. "You seem pretty sure she's going. She has to move up in the standings to get out of New England."

"She will go," Frank said. "I have no doubts. Her free skate is her strength. She skates it on angel's wings."

Sean's red eyebrows disappeared into his hairline. "Angel wings, you say? You sound a wee bit enamored with the girl."

Frank walked around the room, as if Winnie's earlier nervousness had gotten into his system. "It doesn't matter how I feel." He stopped in front of a photograph from perhaps twenty years ago, the girls in long dresses, at an outdoor park. "St. Vrain Skating Clinic" read the engraved title.

"But you do feel something for her. I can tell. I remember how I wept into your boots until the wee hours of the morning before the free skate five years ago, more worried that Maureen wouldn't take me as her husband than on how I would perform."

"I remember. You lost. Which is why I refuse to talk with Winnie about it."

"But I won the important battle. Got meself a wife, something you're still lacking. Does she know how you feel?"

Frank shook his head. "She doesn't know, and she won't, not if I have anything to say about it." He looked at his watch. "She must be done changing by now. She might worry if she can't find me."

"Best of luck to her today. Tell her for me." They left the men's waiting room and headed in opposite directions.

Throughout the afternoon, Frank took Winnie through her warm-up routines, danced with her, the usual things. The entire time his heart kept spinning.

The bell sounded, alerting the final group of women to go onto the ice for warm-ups. She looked at him, panic written across her face.

"I'm praying for you," he said. "Everyone in Maple Notch is praying for you. And up in heaven, your biggest fans, your parents, are watching and cheering. Go out there and skate for them. Skate for the God who is with you, always."

She nodded. Dark bobby pins held her curls in place behind a tan headband, and the cinnamon-colored dress swirled prettily around her legs. With a final hug, he sent her out on the ice.

If she but knew it, his heart went with her.

Chapter 20

Succeed or fail, win or lose, return home in victory or defeat—all would be decided in the next four minutes.

Winnie sucked in her breath, pasted a smile on her face and skated to the center of the ice, throwing kisses to the crowd. They roared, and her smile grew.

Winnie lifted her arms high over her head. Yesterday's debacle disappeared with her soaring first combination jump. The smile on her face became genuine, and she flew through the rest of the program.

She rose out of her final spin to standing crowds, waved and skated to the gate where Frank waited. He grasped her hands in joy. "Pure delight."

One by one, the judges lifted their cards. Four sixes plus 5.8 and 5.9. "What program was that judge looking at?" Frank muttered.

"Shh." Winnie's mind computed the math. She held a commanding lead over the woman who'd gone before her. However, her stiffest competition hadn't yet skated.

"Come ahead. You've done all you can."

The two of them sat in the waiting room as the competition continued, hearing the rumblings of music and cheers. The next skaters whittled Winnie's lead to a scant two points, and if the last skater, the best of the previous day, averaged 5.8s or higher, she would pass Winnie. In that case, Winnie would return to Nationals, but not as the New England champion.

"Look at me." Frank held her hands in a vise, his eyes glittering almost green as they waited through the longest four minutes of her life.

The scores came—5.9, 5.8, 5.6… Winnie's mind scrambled to keep up with the total. It was close, too close.

Frank yanked her to her feet. "You won!"

Frank couldn't stop singing all the way home. The way Winnie had surged from behind to win had made every spill, every minute of practice, all of his self-control, worth it. "Encamped along the hills of light…"

"Please stop singing." Winnie stared out the window. Unlike him, she didn't take pleasure in the win.

Frank stopped in midsong. "What's the problem, Winnie? You won. You got your ticket back to Nationals."

"I'm not going to Nationals." She burrowed her chin into her coat collar.

Frank snapped his head around. "Of course you will. You nailed the free skate. Nationals is just the next step. You might as well make your travel plans for February, because that's where you'll be."

"We can't afford to go to New York. We spent way too much this weekend, and we were just a hop and a skip from home." Her lips turned downward instead of curving up in their usual smile.

"Oh, I have a solution for that." Frank grinned. "I found

us a place to stay for free, plus a meal or two. It won't cost us much at all."

She twisted around and eyed him cautiously. "Where?"

"Sean Rafferty's. He won a silver medal the year I won the gold. He and his wife have a home in New York. We can pick his brain while we're there."

Sean Rafferty. Not quite as good as meeting Sonja Henie, but almost. She didn't know what to say.

"And I won't let you embarrass both of us by refusing the offer."

She knew she was being selfish. All weekend, she had wondered where the faith that had bolstered her up all year had disappeared to. "I know that faith doesn't guarantee a victory in the competition, at least not the kind of victory that results in gold medals. But I was so scared this morning, I felt like I had no faith at all. I deserved to lose."

"I don't know about that. Seems to me, if you don't doubt, there's no room for faith. Sounds contradictory, but it doesn't take faith to believe in something you know for sure."

She hadn't ever thought of it that way.

"So my getting us a place to stay was 'evidence' of my faith that you were going to Nationals," Frank said.

Although the sky was dark when they arrived at the farm, Howie and Arthur ran into the yard as soon as they pulled in. "Hurrah! You won!" Howie shouted.

"Congratulations, Aunt Winnie!" Betty yelled from her bedroom window on the second floor. "Mama let me stay up to say hi. I got to go to bed now. Good night." She ducked inside and shut the window.

Winnie hugged her nephews and headed inside. Clarinda had steaming cups of tea waiting for both of them, along with bowls of hot chicken soup. "I thought you might like something warm to drink after your drive."

She hugged Winnie. "Congratulations. We're all so proud of you."

Winnie had long ago given up wishing her family would attend her competitions. Travel was difficult with young children, and Aunt Flo stayed busy at the Seminary. If her parents still lived, it might be different.

Tonight's celebration was as unexpected as it was welcome, as if the Holy Ghost had told them she'd had a bad weekend and needed some extra encouragement.

When she sat at the table and nibbled on a saltine cracker, Clarinda dug a package out from under the phone table. "This came for you today." She winked at Frank.

Winnie noticed the wink. "What are you two up to?"

"More evidence of faith." Frank smiled enigmatically. "Go ahead, open it."

Winnie refused to be hurried. Three different two-cent stamps appeared on the box, with additional postage. She studied the pictures. One featured the British surrender at Yorktown, another the Red Cross. General Pulaski— she'd test the others on that one. "Who can tell me who General Pulaski was?"

"A Polish count who fought in the Revolutionary War." Of course Clarinda knew the answer. Winnie had remembered the name but not the details.

"Open it," Arthur said.

"All right. Get me a pair of scissors." In order to save the stamps to study later, Winnie cut them out of the upper right-hand corner. She peered at the smudged postmark. "It's from Boston. Did you ask your parents to send me something?"

"I'm not telling." Frank smiled.

She studied the address in the other corner, but no name was given. Howard must know the Sawtelles' address, but from the look on his face, he knew about the surprise. He wouldn't tell.

"Aunt Winnie."

"Very well." She considered untying the string for future use, but the knot was tight, so she cut it. When she removed the paper from the box, she read the inscription of "canned peas." "Someone sent me peas?" She shook the box. "No. Nothing rattles. And it's not all that heavy. Interesting."

Using the scissors, she slit through the tape on one side, then the other, but hesitated with her hands over the top. The Sawtelles had sent her something, something Frank called "evidence of faith." What could it be?

She opened the box, to find tissue paper underneath. Tired of waiting, she tore it away.

Underneath the tissue paper, she found bright red wool with white fluff. She shook it out. It couldn't be…it must be… A skating costume! "It's beautiful!"

Tears fell down her face as she examined the dress: a full, short skirt, a round neck and long sleeves, with white fluff at the wrists and collar, and matching red headband. Inside the box she found a short handwritten note, from Mrs. Sawtelle, which she read aloud. "I know that wool will be warm when you skate inside, but I believe you will skate at an outdoor venue later. My prayer is that the dress will look as beautiful as you skate."

"Go try it on." Clarinda smiled.

Winnie dashed upstairs. The dress slipped on easily, fitting even better than the costume she had worn to the day's competition. And *red,* her favorite color. She turned this way and that, studying herself in the mirror. Faith stormed back, thanks to Frank's thoughtfulness.

She walked to the parlor, where the family had gathered. The skirt, shorter than she wore anywhere except on the ice, made her shy in this environment. Frank's eyes gleamed, and he clapped.

* * *

The alarm clock didn't go off any earlier in the winter than in the summer, but in the dark morning it felt infinitely earlier. Especially on a Monday.

Frank reminded himself they'd have all the time in the world to rest in a few weeks. Four days of practice remained before they had to leave for the national championships in New York City.

Frank wished he could spend a day with his family, to soak up their encouragement. Instead, he and Winnie jogged down the road at a slow pace, their breath coming out in warm puffs. If they ran too fast, the cold would snap at their legs and faces. How did athletes who spent their days on ski slopes keep going in bad weather conditions?

Every now and then a snatch of melody escaped through Winnie's lips as she ran beside him, letting him know what she was thinking about. When she repeated the notes for the phrase "there's something I would tell you if you'll climb a tree with me" several times in a row, he knew she was reviewing that part of the routine. They had analyzed each inch, each twist of the blade, of the arms, the height of her jump. What took a matter of seconds to execute involved endless adjustments.

He wished she had chosen a different song. Every repetition tore at his soul. He wanted to proclaim his love for her, but the time wasn't right.

As they turned a corner, the mill loomed out of the white-on-white world. "Come on. We're almost there. Race you to the door." Winnie threw a handful of snow at him and sprinted ahead.

Wiping off his face, he ran behind her, not too hard, and she arrived first. Laughing, she opened the door, and they entered the darkened building.

Nash poked his head out overhead. "Come on up here before you get started."

Winnie pirouetted with obvious reluctance, her shoes already halfway off her feet. "I need to practice."

"I heard that," Nash said. "This is important."

"Might as well find out what's up." Frank gestured for Winnie to go first, and then he followed along. Nash sat behind his desk, a grin on his face.

"I decided it was time I call in a few favors." Nash pointed to a folder on his desk. The tab read Nationals 1932.

Winnie frowned. What was Preston up to now?

"A couple of things. I talked with a car dealer over in Burlington. He saw you skate t'other night, and he's agreed to lend you a new car to take you to New York. He'd give it to you if times were better, but he'll give you the use of the car for the weekend and money for gas."

"But we have…" Winnie said, but Nash shook his head.

"Mary Anne has kept that Model T running beyond its years long enough. You remember how we almost missed registration last year, when the engine gave us trouble."

Frank's eyebrows rose. He hadn't heard about that bit.

"You need a dependable vehicle. No argument, now." He shook a finger in Winnie's direction.

"You said a couple of things. What else?" Frank asked.

"I got you a corporate sponsor. Greenmont Industries will pay for your entrance fee as well as a small amount for incidental expenses."

Winnie threw her arms around her mentor. "Thank you."

Chapter 21

Frank's head pounded as he trudged home with Winnie late Wednesday night, sledgehammers at his temples and his legs threatening to seize up with every step in the cold.

"A long, hot bath." Winnie sighed.

"You take your bath while I eat hot soup." He would rather collapse into bed, but he needed nourishment, hot water and a chance to examine his leg after the bruising fall he had taken. Winnie's leg was a different matter. "We should get Dr. Landrum to take a look at your leg."

Winnie shook her head. Like most skaters, she called anything short of broken bones a "few bumps and bruises." "It's nothing that a good soak won't take care of."

"You let me be the judge of that." Considering the nature of her fall, he said, "Let your sister take a look."

She scrunched up her face in a frown. "Very well. If you insist."

"I do." Frank was tired of coming down with a heavy hand. One more month, he repeated to himself. Even if she achieved her greatest goal and she went beyond Nationals, the season would end in thirty days.

Let her think he only worried about her physical health and conditioning. Let that smidgeon of animosity that existed between every coach and competitor spur her on to greater heights.

When the house came into view, they picked up their pace. January had brought two weeks of subzero weather.

They fled into the warmth of the kitchen, where Clarinda waited. After they stripped off their winter gear, Winnie headed for the bath. Frank took the bowl of steaming vegetable soup Clarinda had ready.

"You have a letter." She pointed to an envelope on the phone table.

From Mom. He tore it open. "Praise the Lord!"

The baby cried out, and Frank knew he had shouted. "Sorry."

Clarinda shrugged as she stood. "It's time for her next feeding." Touching his shoulder as she passed, she said, "I'll be back soon. I want to hear the news."

After reading the letter, Frank stared at the phone, wishing he could call his parents. But he couldn't justify the expense, and no one welcomed calls at this hour. Instead he steepled his hands together and said a heartfelt prayer of thanks.

He munched a slice of bread with apple butter on it until Winnie and Clarinda returned to the kitchen. Winnie's hair was wet and shiny from shampooing. "The bath is all yours."

The ache in Frank's muscles had faded into the background. "Wait till I tell you the news. They've released Louise from the hospital and say she can come back to the farm. Pa made enough money at the hospital to catch up on the mortgage payments, so they saved the farm." He frowned. "That's the good news. Pa's job goes to someone who has a family member in the hospital. He's out of work. But they'll be here by week's end." He handed the letter to Winnie to read the news for herself, keeping back the last page where they had inquired about Winnie. *Any developments?* Hopefully he could sidetrack that discussion until after they arrived.

"How wonderful!" Winnie spun around as if she was on the ice and winced.

Her grimace reminded Frank of her fall. "Clarinda, you need to take a look at that right thigh of hers. She hit it pretty hard today."

Winnie scowled at him as he left the kitchen and headed for the bath. His right ankle throbbed. He untied his shoes and eased the sock off his foot.

Probing the ankle, he found no broken bones, only a bruised and swollen ligament.

Someone knocked at the door. Winnie said, "I'm leaving a cold compress outside the door."

He hadn't fooled her as well as he had hoped. "What about you?"

"Nothing a couple of aspirin, a good night's rest and some warm-up exercises won't cure. Good night." She rapped on the door to say goodbye and her footsteps faded as she walked away.

Before the cold compress, he would enjoy a good soak. He sprinkled Epsom salts in the water, an investment he considered worth every penny. Later, in his room, he propped his foot on a chair and laid the compress across his ankle. Grabbing his Bible, he turned to the book of Genesis. When not even the enthralling story of Joseph could take his mind off his ankle, he swallowed a couple of aspirin and hobbled to bed.

The following morning, Winnie awoke to closed curtains that blocked out the sky. Her clock lay facedown on the floor, and she had no idea of the time. When she hopped out of bed, she winced as her foot hit the floor. Ignoring it, she checked the window. Pale light appeared on the horizon. She had overslept their usual start time by hours.

What had happened during the night to keep Frank from pounding on the door when she didn't wake up? Even if she had slept through dawn, she doubted if he had.

The first floor was quiet except for the low drone of the Radiola, so Winnie headed for the parlor. Frank and Clarinda sat in the living room. He held the baby in his arms, giving her his finger to hold. Anita chirruped, and Frank laughed. Winnie swallowed. If only she was the one in the rocking chair and Frank was holding their baby...

Nonsense, she reminded herself. He was her coach, with no interest in her beyond making sure she did her best in competition, to claim the gold medal that injury had denied him.

"Aunt Winnie." Norma ran over, and Winnie picked her up.

Frank looked up. "You're awake. Good." He didn't seem in the least upset at the late hour.

"What happened? It's..." She looked at the clock. "Quarter past seven. We should have been at the mill more than two hours ago."

"Not this morning. Today we're having a change of pace, starting with sleeping in."

"You're up, though."

He shrugged. "Not all that long. When I heard the rooster crow, I turned over and went back to sleep for a little bit longer."

"I left you bacon and biscuits in the kitchen. The oatmeal's on the back burner," Clarinda said.

If Frank was giving her a day off, then Winnie would enjoy breakfast. She added a dash of cinnamon sugar to her usual oatmeal while she drank hot coffee and munched on a bacon biscuit. As she rinsed out the bowl, Frank came to the doorway. "Good, you're finished. Go ahead and get ready so we can head out. Be sure and dress warm."

"Yes, sir." She saluted him, intrigued by whatever he had planned for the day.

Instead of heading north toward the mill, he turned the car east toward town and parked by the bridge. She looked at him, puzzled.

"No rehearsals doesn't mean we won't skate. We're going to enjoy it the way God made it possible in the first place, out there on the river. We've been so busy working we've forgotten how to have fun." He handed her their skates and reached for a box behind the seat. "The cave makes it perfect. We can get a fire going to get warm and cook a bite to eat. We'll have the best ice skating party two people can have."

"That sounds like a good idea." Winnie picked her way down the slope, familiar to her from many a childhood camping trip to the cave that had housed her ancestors once upon a time.

She was already tying on her skates when Frank joined her on the riverbank. Cupping her chin with her hand, she studied the smooth ice, and old memories surfaced.

"I remember the very first time I was on ice skates. My parents were there. It's one of the clearest memories I have of them." Winnie had lost them so long ago she didn't think of them all that often. "And your family was there, too. I'm afraid I laughed at Louise when she had trouble skating."

"And I helped the two of you around the ice because Mom and Pa made me do it. I wanted to race with Wallace. Of course, since he was older and bigger, he probably would have won." A smile lit his face. "Are you ready?"

She nodded, and together they glided onto the ice.

Hours passed like minutes, the discomfort from her injury fading as they moved. All too soon Frank called an end to the festivities. They headed for the cave.

"Thank you," Winnie said. "You were right. I remembered why I love to skate. And I didn't fall down once."

"My legs thank you for that." Frank smoothed out the ashes from the fire pit and put their empty dishes back in the box to carry back to the farm. "Tomorrow morning, we'll start extra early."

Winnie groaned. The harsh taskmaster had returned. Days like today teased her with the dream of her and Frank as a couple, but he was all business. In spite of her disappointment, his advice for the day had proven wise. She felt revived, ready to work even harder tomorrow. The car started with hardly a complaint, and they made it back to the farm in a few minutes.

Clarinda met them at the door. "I'm so glad you're back. You have a phone call from New York. A Mr. Rafferty, he said."

"Sean?" Winnie looked at Frank, who shrugged. "I'll take care of our things."

Frank headed for the kitchen.

When she entered the kitchen a few minutes later, Frank was wrapping up the call. "Don't worry about it. We'll be praying for you." Pause. "Of course, I'll let you know."

"Something's happened." The resigned look on Frank's face frightened Winnie. "What is it?"

"Their house burned down. They lost everything. Thank God they were gone, or who knows what else might have happened."

Winnie sunk into the chair. "Oh, the poor man. How awful. Where have they gone?"

"They have a place to stay with his parents until they can figure things out. The thing is, they let the insurance lapse on the house a while back, so they won't get any money."

"Oh, no." No home. Their problems made hers seem insignificant in comparison, but...

Frank frowned apologetically. "Of course I told him we'll be all right, but now we'll need hotel rooms for Nationals."

Chapter 22

As far as Frank was concerned, Saturday came not a moment too soon. He had done his best to assure Winnie that everything would work out. Nash had called the corporate sponsors, to see if they could provide additional help. They hadn't received a response yet, and the wait had taken a toll. The pending return of Frank's family promised refreshment and encouragement that he sorely needed.

The moon hung low in the sky outside the window. Abraham had looked at the same sky when God promised his descendants would be as numerous as the stars in the sky and believed.

"I know I should find that comfort from You, Lord. Forgive me if I like human beings to show it, though." Frank plowed his hands through his hair. To come so close to making it to Nationals, to have every need taken care of… to have it yanked away at the last moment. God's answer would arrive in time. But like Abraham, who tried to rush God by fathering Ishmael, Frank was impatient.

After checking his clock, he padded down the stairs. His family should arrive today, but until then, he and Winnie needed to rehearse. He had the morning planned almost to the minute.

Winnie was cooking their oatmeal when he came in. "What's up with you, sleepyhead?"

"You couldn't sleep either, I take it." Frank accepted the oatmeal she handed to him and leaned against the counter. "Actually, I was thinking about Abraham. About how if God could give his wife a baby when she was ninety, then providing a place for us to sleep for a couple of nights should be easy."

"A week from today." Winnie's voice was distant, as if she was envisioning the arena in New York City. "You have more faith than I do."

"I don't know about that. Let's get going."

The morning passed quickly. At the strike of noon, Louise appeared in the doorway to the mill. She joined Frank at the rail and watched as Winnie completed her turn at the opposite end of the ice.

"Louise!" Winnie broke her routine and skated up the ice, reaching over the sideboards to hug her friend. "You look good."

"I feel so much better." Louise's laughter floated through the air.

Mom and Pa came next, and more greetings were exchanged. "When Clarinda said you were here, we decided to come and see for ourselves."

"Mrs. Sawtelle." Winnie hugged her. "The costume. How can I thank you?"

"I am honored that my humble sewing will be used. You thank me by wearing it."

As much as Frank wanted to visit with his parents, now was not the time. "Speaking of costumes, we have a competition to prepare for."

"Frank, we brought food with us. Can't you stop work for at least a few minutes?"

"Wait until you see what I have planned." He winked and called in a loud voice, "We're ready, Nash." He motioned for Winnie to take her place on the ice.

The music began, Winnie skated in wide, sweeping curves that covered the surface of the ice, building speed for her first jump. As he mouthed the words "and they meant, 'I love you so,'" he gauged her height, her spin— good, but not good enough. He shook his head, and Mom caught the movement.

"Have you told her how you feel?" she asked as Winnie built to a second jump, a combination this time.

He shook his head. "The news about Sean hit us hard. We keep going and going, but I'm not sure how many more rabbits I can pull out of the hat. And it shows. She is skating well, but I feel like she's going through the motions, with no heart."

"Ah, but you're not the one pulling out the rabbits. That's God's job, no?"

"Of course. But I feel responsible."

"Of course you do." Mom patted his hand. "God will provide a way, I am sure. And as for Winnie—" She slapped the railing hard enough that it vibrated against his leg. "Perhaps she needs *you* to skate her best."

The music ended to riotous cheers. Smiling widely, Winnie bowed deeply.

"Or maybe she simply needs an audience to do her best. She looked good to me," Mom said.

Mom's words resurrected a crazy notion that had occurred to Frank at the all–New England competition, but he needed Pa's help. After they finished their meal, Frank invited him outside.

Walking to the car he and Winnie rode in for today, Frank opened the trunk. Holding the small bag in his hands, he questioned his decision. Yes, this was the right thing to do.

He handed the bag to Pa, who peeked inside. "What do you want me to do with *this?*" his father asked.

A smile flickered on Frank's face. "I believe you will approve."

As he explained, a smile widened on Pa's face. "You want this next week, no?"

"By Thursday," Frank said.

Saturday afternoon, after practice and the visit with the Sawtelles, Winnie raced to the soup kitchen. In the weeks since her high school graduation last June, she hadn't missed a day except for competition and the days after Clarinda gave birth. Over the past few months, they had changed her shift to accommodate her new schedule. Practice, soup kitchen, more practice, sleep, repeat it over again.

Unless God did something miraculous in the next five days, she would be here next Saturday as well, instead of skating in New York. She put it out of her mind. This time was reserved for God's work, and the people she helped had worse things to worry about than missing a trip to New York.

As soon as she opened the door, Johnny and Irene ran up to her. "I guess you'll be off to New York City next week, winning that gold medal." Irene held up the newspaper for Winnie to see. The headline read Tuttle Repeats Win at All–New England." Beneath a picture of the mill, it chronicled Preston's conversion of the grist mill into an ice rink and the talent he had discovered in Maple Notch, "with Winifred Tuttle poised to bring the second gold medal in Nationals to our town."

Tears Winnie had promised she wouldn't shed sprang to her eyes.

"What's the matter, Miss Tuttle?" Johnny asked as they walked in.

Danielle came out from behind the kitchen counter. "Has something happened to Louise?"

Winnie shook her head and drew a deep breath. "No. They came to the mill this morning, and she looks good. But we had another setback, and I'm not sure how we're going to get over this one."

"Sit down. Tell me about it."

Winnie stared through the kitchen window, to the pot of stew bubbling on the stove, to the pans of cornbread ready to go in the oven. "I promised myself I wouldn't bring my troubles here."

Danielle planted her hands on her hips. "And why not? We're your friends, or so you say, unless you think you're too good to accept our help?"

That brought a watery chuckle from Winnie. "No, of course not. But compared to what others have to deal with, it's such a small thing."

"Sit down." Danielle joined Winnie on the bench. Olive toddled around behind her, trying to keep up with Eugene. Johnny and Irene sat across from them at the table. "Don't you know how important this championship is, not just to you, but to all of us?" Danielle asked.

Winnie shook her head. "Why should people care?"

"Because you make us believe in dreams. In the future. If you can win—if you can even compete—you give us hope that things will be better for all of us someday. Your faith and perseverance have inspired me to keep going, and I know I speak for others, as well."

The evidence of things not seen…did her skating inspire faith in things not yet seen for the people Winnie so wanted to help? "I never thought of it that way."

"I know it's true, 'cause I heard my ma and pa talking about it," Johnny said. "Pa's got a chance at a job in Burlington that he never would have had, if he hadn't kept on going, just like you."

Winnie threw her arms around the boy and his sister, hugging them close. "I love you both so much." She was crying again, but this time she didn't care. After a few seconds, she let the children go. "Now look at me. I'd better go wash my face and get the cornbread in the oven, or we might not have the meal ready."

Danielle disappeared for a few minutes right before the serving line started, which was uncharacteristic of her. Winnie shrugged it off, cutting the cornbread into squares and slicing pats of butter to put on the plates. Moments before opening the door to the customers who waited in the sanctuary, Danielle reappeared with a young man Winnie recognized as the owner of a small garage on the way to St. Albans.

"Winnie, we wanted you to be the first to know…" Danielle tugged the young man forward. "Herbert asked me to marry him last night, and I said yes." She said it with such rosy-red cheeks that Winnie had to squeal.

Winnie didn't even know they were courting, but she blamed that on her single-minded focus of the past few months. "Oh, I'm so happy for you."

They hugged and parted reluctantly. "We'd better open the door and feed everyone." Danielle turned a pirouette. "But that's hard when you're walking on a cloud."

A few minutes after they started serving, Pastor Rucker gestured for Winnie to join him. "Be back in a minute," she told Danielle and left the kitchen.

"Winnie, there is someone here who is eager to speak with you." The pastor stepped aside, and Winnie saw the reporter who had written the article about the transformed mill.

"Miss Tuttle." He smiled his friendliest smile, and no

reporter notepad was in sight. "Tell me about your latest misfortune in your pursuit of competing at Nationals."

Winnie stared at Danielle, then at the pastor. Who had told the reporter about her problems?

"Why don't you go up to my office." Pastor Rucker led them up the stairs.

Monday afternoon, Frank came to the soup kitchen with Winnie. Pastor Rucker had demanded his presence without explaining why.

"I'm coming with you." Nash joined them in the car after the morning skate. He must know something, or he wouldn't insist.

"I suppose they're planning a celebration of some kind, to wish me well." Winnie seemed puzzled, as well. "Even though we don't know where we're going to stay in New York once we get there. Maybe we'll sleep in the car."

Her laugh sounded strained, and the smile didn't reach her eyes. Her skating had worsened, and he feared that even if they made it to the competition, she wouldn't do her best. But she deserved the chance to at least compete.

To his surprise, people crowded the town square in spite of the cold, and cars and trucks filled the church parking lot. "I guess we can park at the Seminary. Aunt Flo won't mind." Winnie peered over her shoulder. "I wonder what is going on."

Frank peeked at Nash, who sat motionless. He knew the reason, but he wasn't telling.

As they walked around the square, a cheer greeted them. A large crowd had gathered on the church lawn, with Irene and Johnny holding up a banner. "Good luck, Winnie Tuttle! We love you!" Crude drawings of gold, silver and bronze medals on red, white and blue ribbons decorated the banner. The one that had greeted Frank's July homecoming was fancier, but he preferred the heartfelt sentimentality of this one. Frank had won a medal, but Winnie held the hearts of the people of Maple Notch in her hands.

The banner stretched over a table scattered with baked goods, crocheted hat and mitten sets, clothing, knick-knacks of every sort, pots and pans, toys and books. Most of it was scuffed and worn, with a few new items visible here and there. The town hadn't seen a sale like this since Black Tuesday, and they never held one in the middle of January.

Large sections of the table lay bare, and plates bearing baked goods had emptied. The sale had been in progress for some time and a lot had sold.

A man stepped in front of them with a camera. "Smile!" A flash popped in their eyes. "Did you see the special edition of the paper?"

Frank shook his head. "Just your regular weekly edition, last Saturday."

"Here it is." Nash pulled the paper out of his coat and handed it to Frank. Danielle gave Winnie an identical page.

Golden Dreams Threatened the headline screamed from above the fold. A picture of Winnie, wearing a stained apron, smiled at him. The caption read, "Winnie Tuttle volunteers at the church's soup kitchen six days a week."

The first paragraph answered the five W's about their dream of national and international competition, and described the latest disaster that stood in their way.

When Frank unfolded the paper, his own image stared back at him, as well as several more pictures of Winnie. Scanning the lines of the article, he saw that someone had filled the reporter in on the string of misfortunes they had endured over the course of the past six months.

A text box in the middle of the center column said, "For information on how you can help Winifred Tuttle compete in New York this week, look on the next page."

Small ads from every business in town framed the text. The article detailed an emergency sale to be held daily until they had raised sufficient funds for the trip. People wishing to donate goods were encouraged to bring them early, and buyers were asked to return often. A final asterisk indicated that all the fees from the advertisements would be given to the fund.

Winnie's hand slipped into Frank's, and she smiled at him as if she couldn't believe it.

Evidence of things unseen, indeed.

Chapter 23

Thursday morning, Winnie stared out the window. Sleep had eluded her in the early dawn as she wondered if her unbelievable, impossible trip to Nationals would end any differently than last year. Would all the effort, hope, preparation—faith—have tangible results?

Her suitcase lay packed, her beautiful red costume carefully wrapped. She had lingered in the bathtub last night, no more able to get to sleep than she could stay asleep this morning. The loaner car sat in the front yard, bathed in the last rays of moonlight. She opened her Bible to the concordance at the back and looked up a few verses on faith, since that had been the message God kept sending to her all year.

Habakkuk said it first, and later Paul repeated it to the Romans: The just shall live by his faith. She figured she had done her share of living by faith this year. "According to your faith be it unto you." Jesus said that one. In that case, her faith had wavered.

Enough. She had practiced and prayed, and she didn't know where her faith ended and her doubts started. If she continued skating the way she had in recent practices, she didn't deserve to win. Whatever happened, God would work together for her good. Her alarm went off at last, and she tucked her Bible into her suitcase. She donned a warm woolen dress, wanting to look like a champion when she arrived, no matter how rumpled she felt.

By the time she and Frank finished their oatmeal, the entire family had gathered, including Wallace's family and the Sawtelles. Frank carried their bags out to the car and tarried to speak privately with his father.

Preston came to the door, carrying his duffel bag. "I couldn't let you go to New Yawk without me taggin' along." Winnie's heart lifted. The money raised allowed for three of them to travel, and she was glad Preston had agreed to come with them.

As the family walked with her to the waiting loan car, Mary Anne said, "I'm glad you didn't have to risk the Model T. I tinkered with it, but this car is safer. You even have a spare tire and chains." She was a wonder with machines, and Winnie trusted her judgment.

Winnie and Frank worked their way around the circle, hugging each person. "Are you sure the baby should be out in this weather?" Winnie asked Clarinda. Anita still looked tiny.

"She'll be fine." Clarinda shifted the baby to her other arm and hugged her sister.

Winnie lifted Norma and swung her around.

"Hurry back," her niece said.

"Here's a rabbit's foot, for good luck." Howie handed it over.

Wallace hugged Winnie tight before she stepped back.

"We're only going away for a few days. Why all the fuss?"

"Because when you come back, you're not going to be my little sister anymore," Wallace said, "but a national gold medalist."

Frank and Winnie reached Louise at the same moment, and the three of them embraced. "You two take care of each other."

"We will." Frank's voice sounded like a low, deep bell.

A car scraped over the ice before stopping, and Pastor Rucker stepped out, with Danielle and Aunt Flo emerging from the passenger side.

After they said their goodbyes, Pastor Rucker led the group in prayer, and Frank and Winnie climbed into the car.

Frank cranked the motor. Grinning, he said, "Next stop, New York City."

Frank stared sightlessly out the restaurant window, giving Winnie time to eat as much as she could stomach. He couldn't stand to watch her pick at her food. Of the three of them, only Nash ate with a normal appetite.

"I'm finished." Winnie pushed aside her plate, and Frank looked at it. She had managed to eat the chicken breast and fresh salad, leaving only a small crust of bread uneaten. Probably she ate more out of her desire not to waste food they had purchased than out of hunger.

Nash stretched and yawned. "I'm goin' up to the room for a spell. You two might have a hankerin' to explore the city."

Frank nodded. "After all that sitting, I need to stretch my legs. Want to take a look at New York with me, Winnie? Maybe go see the world's tallest building?"

Winnie's eyes lit up. "Would we have time to go to the Statue of Liberty? When I came to New York with Wallace and Mary Anne five years ago, we didn't get there."

Frank had heard the stories about that trip, which had included the mob kidnapping Mary Anne.

"Let's find out." They paid the bill and checked a map. "Where shall we go first?"

Winnie craned her neck up, up, pointing to the skyscraper he had mentioned. "We can walk to the Empire State Building from here. Let's do that first."

They walked into the lobby to the elevator. The ride would cost a coin, but the expense was worth it. He'd do anything to take Winnie's mind off the competition, to clear her worries and prepare her for tomorrow.

"Why one hundred and two stories, I wonder? And not one hundred."

Frank shrugged. "Maybe the next tallest building already had one hundred stories."

At last they reached the observation deck and walked to the parapet. "I believe that's our hotel. Look." Winnie pointed and leaned over, and Frank resisted the urge to pull her back.

"I can see just fine from here." So many buildings were spread below them, and the sky was so close, an airplane might zoom toward them and crash into the building.

"We're so high in the sky, I feel like I could see Maple Notch if the day was clear."

Frank tired of the sight sooner than Winnie did, but at last they descended to street level. They caught the wrong bus, heading north instead of south, and had to cover the length of Manhattan to reach Battery Park. By the time they arrived, they had missed the last ferry.

Winnie rested her elbows on the railing as dusk slowly shrouded the statue. "I guess I'm just not meant to see her up close. This is my second trip to New York. I don't know if I'll ever be here again."

Frank wished he could promise her a return trip. "If

you reach your goal, you might get to travel to encourage figure skating around the world."

She laughed. "I'll leave that to Sonja Henie." She walked along the railing, running her hand over the smooth metal, until they reached a plaque. "There used to be artillery batteries here, to protect the fledgling settlement. From what, it doesn't say. Who did they expect to come at them over the water?"

Frank stared across the harbor, imagining it with only a handful of buildings behind him and danger surrounding them. "I don't know, maybe Indians in canoes? Later there were the British, of course."

Winnie had continued her walk around the park. "I always read these things. Aunt Flo taught us to read every description of every piece. This one says that people came here on Evacuation Day at the end of the Revolutionary War, when the last British troops left American soil." She glanced at Frank.

If he closed his eyes and concentrated, shouts turned into war cries. The waves crashing against the shore became the roar of cannons and the smooth metal beneath his fingers mimicked the barrel of a musket. How brave those Americans were, taking on the British Empire—and winning. Incredible. Fueled by passion, faith and patriotism, they won an impossible victory.

"If they could win against such impossible odds, I suppose I can, too," Winnie said. "After all, my great-great-whatever fought with Ethan Allen and the Green Mountain Boys."

Frank glanced at his watch. The day's driving was catching up with him. "It's time to head back to the hotel. Tomorrow will come early."

After a long grueling day of competition on Friday, Winnie left the ice disheartened. At the end of the compulsory figures she stood in sixth place, lower than last year. She hadn't embarrassed herself, but she hadn't improved, either. Waiting until she reached the waiting room to wilt, she sank onto a chair and folded over, hugging her knees.

A shadow appeared in front of her.

"Go away." Her voice came out in a low growl.

"Get up." Frank's voice landed gently on her ears. "We have work to do tonight."

Work. Of course. When did he ever ask anything else of her? "It won't make a difference. Either I'm ready or I'm not."

"I'm trying something new. Come on." He held out his hand. "Do you trust me? Absolutely?"

"Yes." Without hesitation, she grabbed his hand. Hard taskmaster he might be, demanding, pushy—but did she consider him trustworthy? With every fiber of her being, provided she could keep a guard around her heart.

He smiled. "Good."

After saying a few gracious words to the women in the top five, Winnie walked out of the arena with Frank. "Where is Preston?" She couldn't imagine her mentor deserting her at this time, when he must know the depth of her disappointment. *Unless he was disappointed in her, as well.* She wanted to cry.

"I told him I needed this time alone with you, and he agreed. We'll catch up with him later."

When had Preston ever been absent from her dealings with Frank?

Frank patted her hand. "I'm trying a different approach. We're going to Good Shepherd Church, Mary Anne's home church."

"But they can't have…"

"No, they don't have ice. But we don't need it for what I have planned." If she could trust her eyes, the look he gave her seemed tender.

They left the skating equipment at the hotel before heading to the church, and Pastor Asher greeted them at the door. "I am so glad you called. Mary Anne has told us of Miss Tuttle's accomplishments, and I have followed your career with interest. I am happy that we can assist in some way." He led them to the church basement, much like the one in Maple Notch where she served meals six days a week. Aside from two chairs, the room was empty. It wasn't quite as large as the ice, but it was adequate.

Bone tired and soul-deep discouraged, Winnie didn't know how much good rehearsal would accomplish, but Frank would not be denied. "Okay. What do you need me to do?"

He rewarded her with another tender, brilliant smile. "Nothing. I'm going to do something for you. Something I should have done long ago, except I thought it would distract you from your goal."

Then why do it now, less than twenty-four hours before her fate was decided?

"I'm going to explain the choreography to you," he said.

"But I know the steps." The objection came out before she could stop it. "I'm sorry."

"Ah, but you don't know what was going through my mind when we did it."

Winnie recalled their conversation on that September day after the horrible episode when she burned her skates. What stood out was the hope, the joy—the amazing feeling of being in Frank's arms when they danced. Since then, that emotion had plunged to the bottom of the Arctic Ocean and her performance along with it. Intrigued by the idea, she sat back in the chair and crossed her legs. "I'm listening."

"You chose the song that I liked best. Not because of its suitability for skating—others might have been better for that—but because of its subject—a couple who had known each other forever who fell in love."

Winnie colored. "It's just a song."

Frank simply smiled and hummed a few notes. "'I've come to see the little girl I loved from year to year, I've come to watch each little curl that made your head so dear.'"

His hand reached out and lifted a curl that fell over her forehead. "Your hair has always been so curly."

He liked her impossibly curly hair?

"'Let's go out to the orchard where we roamed in childish glee, There's something I would tell you if you'll climb a tree with me.'" He grinned. "Do you remember climbing up the tree at the fishing hole before we jumped in the water?"

Wide-eyed, she nodded.

Instead of singing the chorus, he began the second verse. "'I've left the noisy city with its heartaches and its strife to make you happy sweetheart in the noon time of your life.'" His eyes pierced. "I didn't come back to Maple Notch because Howard offered me a job. I wanted to make you happy."

Winnie started to cry.

"'Success was hard to win dear. At last it came to me. I'll tell you all about it if you climb the tree with me.'" He tugged his medal out of his pocket and dangled it before throwing it in the air where it glinted in the light. "Hard to win and easily lost."

What was he saying…?

"'Oh come and climb a tree with me, as we climbed so long ago. All the birds sang birdie words, and they meant "I love you so."'" He pulled her to her feet. "By September I knew I was falling in love with you."

Her lips parted, but he shut them with a finger as he pulled her close, leading her in the three-step waltz.

"You're still the girl with a curl, and I've tired of city life. I'd be happy to spend the rest of my days with you, even if it's in a tree."

Leaning forward, he captured her lips in a kiss, leaving her too breathless to answer.

Chapter 24

On free-skate Saturday, Winnie slept in, resting more soundly than she had for weeks. She had floated home from the church on air, certain she wouldn't close her eyes. But when she did, sleep followed quickly.

A knock rapped on her door, and she flew to open it. Preston stood there. "Forget I was in New Yawk, did you?"

She crossed her arms. "You *knew.*"

"Anyone with a pair of eyes could see how he felt about you. Just took a kick in the pants to get him to tell you about it."

She giggled. "I'm so happy."

He laid a hand on her shoulder. "I pray that happiness inside translates to the free skate of your life. Go out there and claim it, girl. You earned it." Preston seldom spoke so much, or so directly. When she hugged him, he shrugged away, as if uncomfortable.

Frank entered the hall, his face breaking into a smile when he saw Winnie. "Are you ready?"

"Always." She giggled at the word.

Even with a leisurely breakfast, they arrived at the arena well before their required check-in time of noon. Because of her sixth-place finish, Winnie would skate in the last group, and she received the good news that she would skate last.

Winnie changed into her costume, her skin tingling as she pulled on the tights, the dress slipping softly over her skin. Checking the mirror, trying to decide whether or not to apply makeup, she was surprised to see her cheeks weren't as bright as her costume. Now she could benefit from Mary Anne's skilled hand. Her sister-in-law no longer dolled up the way she did in her wild flapper days, but she had a good eye for color and skin.

Simplest was best. Winnie applied red lipstick to match the bright dress color and the headband that held her hair away from her eyes. God must have known she'd love red when He gave her dark hair and eyes.

After she had finished her toilette, she came into the waiting room. Frank's smiling nod gave his approval. "Are you ready to warm up?" Taking her assent for granted, he led her through exercises that loosened her muscles enough to skate without strain.

The final group competition began, and Frank held her hands while each score was announced. The scores rose higher and higher. When the fourth score was announced—the leader from the previous day—she had earned such a high score that only perfect scores from Winnie would win.

Frank held her face between his hands gently. "Success was hard to win, my dear, but at last it will come to you." He whispered against her lips, not quite kissing them. Joy flooded into Winnie's heart, and peace settled on her. Win, medal or finish even lower than yesterday—she had won the most important battle.

She stood, the song running through her mind, turning and twisting and reviewing the steps as the fifth skater went. Before she knew it, the clerk motioned her onto the ice for her brief warm-up while the judges made their final decisions for the previous skater.

"Winifred Tuttle, skating to 'Climb a Tree With Me' by Charles Harris."

Winnie reached center ice and lifted her hands over her head.

The music began, and she glided across the ice on the same cloud that had taken her home from the church last night.

Each note, each letter, each remembered word—each step of the skates, each kick of the legs and jump in the air—flowed together like a summer zephyr, airy, light, moving.

The music ended and she came out of her daze. The scores confirmed what she knew in her heart.

She'd won the gold medal at the United States Figure Skating Championships—and she was going to represent the United States in international competition.

Frank cheered louder than anyone else as the gold medal was draped around Winnie's neck. He thought one of the bystanders had knocked into him when a man's voice spoke directly behind him. "Mr. Sawtelle, I would like to have a word with you when you are available."

The voice belonged to Boyce Raider, the man who had championed ice skating in New England for longer than Frank had been alive. When he turned around, Raider handed him a business card. "Come see me before you leave. Anyone who can prepare a skater for competition the way you prepared Miss Tuttle deserves recognition. I want to talk with you about a job."

With that unexpected statement, Raider disappeared back into the crowd. Frank had just been handed the final piece to his dreams.

"Are you sure you want to do this?" Winnie clung to Frank's hand, and he grazed her knuckles with his lips. They waited at the edge of the ice, ready for the Sunday-afternoon exhibitions.

"I dressed for it." He looked down at the black pants Mr. Raider had supplied, and the red-and-tan flannel shirt he had brought from home, the only thing that matched Winnie's outfit. "Mr. Raider wants to make a big splash with his announcement. Since I'm going to work for him, I need to do as he says." He grinned at her. "Don't worry, I won't do anything to hurt myself."

The wiggles inside of Winnie kept escaping, and she couldn't keep still.

Within the past thirty-six hours, Frank had declared his love for her, she had won a national championship and he had landed a job as an assistant coach in Raider's organization. Such an unexpected total victory was sweet, indeed.

Preston came up behind them. "I thought you might be needin' this." He handed Frank his gold medal and pointed to the one hanging from Winnie's neck. "You've got a matched pair, except for the date." He slipped Frank a small package that he tucked into the waistband of his leggings.

Frank squeezed Winnie's hand.

"Today's audience is in for a special treat. Appearing together for the first time on the ice, please welcome our new women's gold medalist, Winifred Tuttle, and the man who earned his title five years ago, Frank Sawtelle."

Applause grew wild as they glided onto the ice together.

"Together they are skating to a song they claim is the

secret to their success. 'Faith is the Victory.' Instead of a recording, our band will play for them."

Although only planned last night, the performance was as polished as those of many of the seasoned pairs skaters. If the first time Winnie had skated with Frank had been wonderful, this transported her directly into dreamland. At the end of the first chorus, "Oh, glorious victory!" they landed perfect side-by-side jumps. The second time through, Frank held her arms in a gravity-defying spin. The crowd applauded every nuance, every trick that they performed.

When the band slid into a final amen, Frank and Winnie spun in unison, ending at the exact moment the music faded away.

The crowd surged to their feet. Frank joined his hand with hers, lifting it high into the air, and the noise grew louder.

Frank motioned for the microphone and waited for the noise to subside. Winnie looked at him, puzzled.

"Faith and victory. Our country needs both things as we go through these trying times. After injury ended my days in competition, I needed faith that any kind of victory was possible."

Someone in the crowd called out "You never skated better" amid renewed applause.

"That's when God brought a special woman into my life, who also happened to be a spectacular skater."

Clapping again interrupted.

"Through her eyes, I learned that when we trust God for the important things—like helping others and family and love—He takes care of everything else. And so here, in front of our wonderful skating fans, I'm going to take a risk on one final victory."

Smiling, he went to his knees on the ice while fishing in his waistband. He drew out a small red velvet box that could only contain a ring. Winnie put a hand to her throat while the crowd sank into silence, holding their collective breath.

"I gave my father the gold statue I won five years ago and asked him to take it to a jeweler to fashion a ring—a ring with ice skates etched into the band—one that represents our past and our future." He opened the box and Winnie could see the beauty of the design, as well as the small diamond mounted between two skates.

"Winifred Tuttle, will you do me the honor of becoming my wife?"

"Say yes!" A hundred voices from the crowd urged her.

She leaned close to the mic, so that her voice would carry. "With all my heart."

The couple kissed. When they broke apart, they faced first one side of the arena, then the other, waving while flashbulbs recorded the event for the world.

The headline of the following edition of the *Maple Notch Gazette* read Skaters to Wed.

In a photograph big enough to fill half the columns on the page, a smiling Winnie and Frank stood side by side. Gold medals hung from each neck, and Winnie held up her left hand, where a diamond ring glittered.

* * * * *

Author's Note

In planning an international-level figure skating story set in the United States, I had only one choice prior to World War II: the 1932 Winter Games held in Lake Placid, New York. In 1932 Sonja Henie won the second of her three consecutive Olympic figure skating championships; as much as I wanted my heroine, Winnie Tuttle, to win gold, I decided not to touch Henie's still-unbroken record.

The actual first-place skater at the 1932 Nationals was Maribel Vinson. She held the title for most of the ten years between 1928 and 1937, broken only once, by Suzanne Davis in 1934. Five years earlier, Nathaniel Niles won the men's championship, not Frank Sawtelle.

SPECIAL EXCERPT FROM

Love Inspired

He was her high school crush, and now he's a single father of twins. Allison True just got a second chance at love.

Read on for a sneak preview of
STORYBOOK ROMANCE by Lissa Manley,
the exciting fifth book in
THE HEART OF MAIN STREET series,
available October 2013.

Something clunked from the back of the bookstore, drawing Allison True's ever-vigilant attention. Her ears perking up, she rounded the end of the front counter. Another clunk sounded, and then another. Allison decided the noise was coming from the Kids' Korner, so she picked up the pace and veered toward the back right part of the store, creasing her brow.

She arrived in the area set up for kids. Her gaze zeroed in on a dark-haired toddler dressed in jeans and a red shirt, slowly yet methodically yanking books off a shelf, one after the other. Each book fell to the floor with a heavy clunk, and in between each sound, the little guy laughed, clearly enjoying the sound of his relatively harmless yet messy play.

Allison rushed over, noting there was no adult in sight. "Hey, there, bud," she said. "Whatcha doing?"

He turned big brown eyes fringed with long, dark eyelashes toward her. He looked vaguely familiar even though she was certain she'd never met this little boy.

"Fun!" A chubby hand sent another book crashing to the floor. He giggled and stomped his feet on the floor in a little happy dance. "See?"

Carefully she reached out and stilled his marauding hands. "Whoa, there, little guy." She gently pulled him away. "The books are supposed to stay on the shelf." Holding on to him, she cast her gaze about the enclosed area set aside for kids, but her view was limited by the tall bookshelves lined up from the edge of the Kids' Korner to the front of the store. "Are you here with your mommy or daddy?"

The boy tugged. "Daddy!" he squealed.

"Nicky!" a deep masculine voice replied behind her. "Oh, man. Looks like you've been making a mess."

A nebulous sense of familiarity swept through her at the sound of that voice. Not breathing, still holding the boy's hand, Allison slowly turned around. Her whole body froze and her heart gave a little spasm then fell to her toes as she looked into deep brown eyes that matched Nicky's.

Sam Franklin. The only man Allison had ever loved.

Pick up STORYBOOK ROMANCE
in October 2013 wherever Love Inspired® Books are sold.

LIEXP0913

REQUEST YOUR FREE BOOKS!

2 FREE CHRISTIAN NOVELS
PLUS 2
FREE
MYSTERY GIFTS

HEARTSONG
PRESENTS

YES! Please send me 2 Free Heartsong Presents novels and my 2 FREE mystery gifts (gifts are worth about $10). After receiving them, if I don't wish to receive any more books I can return the shipping statement marked "cancel." If I don't cancel, I will receive 4 brand-new novels every month and be billed just $4.24 per book in the U.S. and $5.24 per book in Canada. That's a savings of at least 20% off the cover price. It's quite a bargain! Shipping and handling is just 50¢ per book in the U.S. and 75¢ per book in Canada.* I understand that accepting the 2 free books and gifts places me under no obligation to buy anything. I can always return a shipment and cancel at any time. Even if I never buy another book, the two free books and gifts are mine to keep forever.

159/359 HDN FVYK

Name	(PLEASE PRINT)
Address	Apt. #
City	State	Zip

Signature (if under 18, a parent or guardian must sign)

Mail to the Harlequin® Reader Service:
IN U.S.A.: P.O. Box 1867, Buffalo, NY 14240-1867

* Terms and prices subject to change without notice. Prices do not include applicable taxes. Sales tax applicable in N.Y. This offer is limited to one order per household. Not valid for current subscribers to Heartsong Presents books. All orders subject to credit approval. Credit or debit balances in a customer's account(s) may be offset by any other outstanding balance owed by or to the customer. Please allow 4 to 6 weeks for delivery. Offer available while quantities last. Offer valid only in the U.S.

Your Privacy—The Harlequin® Reader Service is committed to protecting your privacy. Our Privacy Policy is available online at www.ReaderService.com or upon request from the Harlequin Reader Service.
We make a portion of our mailing list available to reputable third parties that offer products we believe may interest you. If you prefer that we not exchange your name with third parties, or if you wish to clarify or modify your communication preferences, please visit us at www.ReaderService.com/consumerchoice or write to us at Harlequin Reader Service Preference Service, P.O. Box 9062, Buffalo, NY 14269. Include your complete name and address.

HSPDIR13R

HEARTSONG
PRESENTS

Look out for 4 new
Heartsong Presents books next month!

Every month 4 inspiring faith-filled
romances will be available in stores.

These contemporary and historical Christian
romances emphasize God's role in every
relationship and reinforce the importance of
faith, hope and love.

Eve Pickering knows what it's like to be judged because of your past. So she's not about to leave the orphaned boy she's befriended alone and unprotected in this unfamiliar Texas town. And if Chance Dawson's offer of shelter is the only way she can look after Leo, Eve will turn it into a warm, welcoming home for the holidays. No matter how temporary it may be—or how much she's really longing to stay for good....

Chance came all the way from the big city to make it on his own in spite of his secret...and his overbearing rich family. But Eve's bravery and caring is giving him a confidence he never expected— and a new direction for his dream. And with a little Christmas luck, he'll dare to win her heart as well as her trust—and make their family one for a lifetime.

Texas Grooms

A Family for Christmas

by

WINNIE GRIGGS

Available October 2013 wherever
Love Inspired Historical books are sold.

LIH82983

Love Inspired.
SUSPENSE
RIVETING INSPIRATIONAL ROMANCE

FALL FROM GRACE by MARTA PERRY
Teacher Sara Esch helps widower Caleb King comfort his daughter who witnessed a crime. But then Sara gets too close to the truth and Caleb must risk it all for the woman who's taught him to love again.

DANGEROUS HOMECOMING by DIANE BURKE
Katie Lapp needs her childhood friend Joshua Miller more than ever when someone threatens her late husband's farm. Katie wants it settled the Amish way...but not everyone can be trusted. Can Joshua protect her...even if it endangers his heart?

RETURN TO WILLOW TRACE by KIT WILKINSON
Lydia Stoltz wants to avoid the man who courted her years ago. But a series of accidents startles their Plain community...and leads her straight to Joseph Yoder. At every turn, it seems their shared past holds the key to their future.

DANGER IN AMISH COUNTRY,
a 3-in-1 anthology including novellas by
MARTA PERRY, DIANE BURKE and
KIT WILKINSON

Available October 2013 wherever
Love Inspired Suspense books are sold.

LIS44558R